He held on to Andrea with all his strength, hoping that maybe the two of them together could will away any future problems for Dani, even while knowing they were powerless.

Life happened. It just did. There was no good luck charm to ward off bad events or illnesses, or parents letting their kids go into foster care…no way to skip around the messy parts.

As they stood holding each other it hit Sam how, without even realizing it, they'd become a kind of family where Dani was concerned. Did he love her? Even if he *did* think he might love Andrea, being a reasonable man, he still couldn't believe it was possible yet. Was he ready to tell her something he wasn't even sure he was capable of?

Plus, he had Dani now. There would be two broken hearts if things didn't work out. Yet Dani had fallen for Andrea right off, and kids were usually pretty good judges of character. Which brought his thoughts full circle to Andrea, the woman in his arms, who'd gone all weepy worrying about his son. Yeah, they'd become a modern-day melded family whether they were ready for it or not.

Those astoun... ...ezing her eve... ...his happen... ...

Dear Reader,

Writers are often asked where they get their ideas for stories. I can tell you I get mine all over the place! The spark that spurred *A Mother for His Adopted Son* came from an article about an ocularist in a regional magazine I subscribe to from Maine. I'd never heard of the profession, and was fascinated by this woman who'd been an art student but for the last thirty years had wound up making beautiful prosthetic eyes for clients. I clipped and held on to that article for a couple of years and it percolated in the back of my mind.

Another day, I was driving around doing errands and listening to the radio when an intriguing interview aired, about a sightless man who had become amazingly independent through using a technique called echolocation. The interviewer began by describing this man as having beautiful blue eyes and, yes, they were prosthetics. He'd lost both his eyes by the time he was eighteen months old to retinoblastoma, but his mother never let his blindness hold him back from exploring and being adventurous. That sparked my dormant ocularist idea and, as they say, a story kernel was created!

An ocularist isn't a 'usual' job for a Medical Romance character, so I ran it by my editor, who was open and encouraging about the idea. Soon the character Andrea came to be, and shortly after that a little boy named Dani, too. But who would be the hero of this story, and why? It didn't take long for the gorgeous pediatrician Dr Sammy to come into being—a dedicated doctor who believes in medical missions and adoption for very personal reasons.

I hope you enjoy the dramatic and often emotional love story between Andrea and Sam as they work their way to their happily-ever-after.

I always enjoy hearing from readers at lynnemarshall.com. And 'friend' me on Facebook at www.facebook.com/LynneMarshall.Page!

Love,

Lynne

A MOTHER
FOR HIS
ADOPTED SON

BY
LYNNE MARSHALL

MILLS
BOON

Published in Great Britain 2016
By Mills & Boon, an imprint of HarperCollins*Publishers*
1 London Bridge Street, London, SE1 9GF

© 2016 Janet Maarschalk

ISBN: 978-0-263-25424-2

Our policy is to use papers that are natural, renewable and recyclable
products and made from wood grown in sustainable forests. The logging
and manufacturing processes conform to the legal environmental
regulations of the country of origin.

Printed and bound in Spain
by CPI, Barcelona

Lynne Marshall used to worry that she had a serious problem with daydreaming—and then she discovered she was supposed to write those stories! Being a late bloomer, she came to fiction-writing after her children were grown. Now she battles the empty nest by writing stories which include romance, medicine, and always a happily-ever-after. She is a Southern California native, a woman of faith, a dog lover, and a curious traveller.

Books by Lynne Marshall

Mills & Boon Medical Romance

Cowboys, Doctors...Daddies!

Hot-Shot Doc, Secret Dad
Father for Her Newborn Baby

Temporary Doctor, Surprise Father
The Boss and Nurse Albright
The Heart Doctor and the Baby
The Christmas Baby Bump
Dr Tall, Dark...and Dangerous?
NYC Angels: Making the Surgeon Smile
200 Harley Street: American Surgeon in London

Visit the Author Profile page
at millsandboon.co.uk for more titles.

To foster parents and adoptive parents worldwide,
who open their homes and hearts
and make a difference in young lives.

Praise for
Lynne Marshall

'Heartfelt emotion that will bring you to the point of
tears, for those who love a second-chance romance
written with exquisite detail.'
—*Contemporary Romance Reviews* on
NYC Angels: Making the Surgeon Smile

'Lynne Marshall contributes a rewarding story to the
NYC Angels series, and her gifted talent repeatedly
shines. *Making the Surgeon Smile* is an outstanding
romance with genuine emotions and passionate
desires.'

—*CataRomance*

CHAPTER ONE

SAM MARCUS STOOD in the observation room above the OR suite in St. Francis of the Valley Hospital, waiting for his child to lose an eye. He'd seen his share of surgeries before, being a pediatrician, but never for someone he loved. This time he needed an anchor, so he leaned against the window to see his son better and to offer support against the threat of his buckling knees.

He watched as the anesthesiologist put his tiny boy under and while the surgeon measured the eye globe and cornea dimensions, the length of the optic nerve. His heart thumped in his chest, and a fine line of sweat gathered above his lip as the surgeon made the first incision. He swiped it away with a trembling hand, trying his best to get his mind wrapped around what was happening.

Enucleation.

His barely three-year-old newly adopted son had retinoblastoma and needed to have his left eye surgically removed. He swallowed hard and shook his head, still unable to believe it.

He'd fallen in love with Danilo, an orphan, on his last Doctors' Medical Missions trip to the Philippines. The mission had been in response to their latest typhoon, to tend to the countless new orphans. He hadn't been in the market for a son or daughter. No, it had been the last thing on his mind then. Yet there had been one particular one-year-old boy who'd lost his entire family in the typhoon and who'd miraculously managed to survive for forty-eight hours on his own. A little hero.

Over the days of the two-week mission, Sam and the other doctors had performed physicals and minor procedures, as well as arranged for other children who had required more extensive medical care to be transported to where they needed to be. Dani had used his new walking skills to follow Sam everywhere. It'd made Sam remember one of his favorite childhood books, *Are You My Mommy?* A story his own mother had read to him, where a little bird who'd fallen out of the nest went looking for his mother, asking everyone, even machines, if they were his mother, and it had broken his heart.

All the children on this mission were orphans dealing with their losses in their own ways, yet this child, Dani, seemed to have chosen Sam. He gave in and took the boy with him everywhere at the orphanage clinic, cautiously opened his heart, then fell in love in an amazingly short period of time. Then it was time to leave. Dani cried inconsolably, and one of the sisters at the orphanage told Sam that it was the first time the child had cried since arriving there six weeks before.

What was a man supposed to do? He knew how it felt to be homeless. He'd been taken away from his mother when he was ten. She hadn't abused him, but she'd had to leave him alone most nights so she could work a second job. Her plan had backfired and the authorities had taken Sam and put him into foster care. Yeah, he knew how it felt to be left all alone.

Fortunately for him he'd been placed into a big happy family and currently suffered from missing them, with everyone fanned out all across the United States. There'd been five natural siblings in all, and he'd become kid number six, yet his already overworked foster mother had insisted on bringing in more foster children—a long, long list of foster kids had come and gone over the years. *Why?* he used to ask whenever he'd been instructed to share his bunk bed with yet another new kid. *We don't have room for more, Mom.* She'd always insisted he call her Mom.

Even after all these years her response never left his subconscious. "We don't always know how we'll make ends meet or where they'll sleep, Sammy, but we just know we've got to bring them in because the child needs a home."

The child needs a home.

He'd been one of those children. And he'd been trying to prove himself worth keeping ever since.

When he'd returned home from the Philippines, he'd been unable to get Dani out of his mind. Missing his infectious smile and unconditional love, he'd decided to try for the adoption in honor of his deceased foster mother, because that child needed a home.

Though it had taken a year and a half to jump through all the hoops to arrange for Dani's adoption, six months ago he and Dani had teamed up and never looked back. And what an adjustment being a single father had been. It'd always been hectic, growing up with so many foster siblings, yet under the chaos there had been stability. Something he'd never had when he'd been a young boy. That was his goal for Dani, to give the boy stability, but he'd never been a parent before and they were both on a stiff learning curve, working things out, juggling the logistics of his busy career, child care and father-son time.

Then this cancer nightmare had happened, and any stability they'd established had been replaced with utter mental and emotional turmoil.

They'd discovered the tumor on Dani's very first eye examination in the United States. The simple yet disturbing fact that his pupil had turned white instead of red when the ophthalmologist had shone a light into it had heralded the beginning of more and more bad news. The child had intraocular retinoblastoma.

The team of doctors, headed by the pediatric oncologist, had recommended the surgery after all other avenues of treatment—each with drawbacks and no guarantees—had been considered and rejected. Dr. Van Diesel, the pediatric eye surgeon, had come highly recommended, and since there wasn't a chance that Dani's vision could be saved, they'd opted for enucleation.

Sam watched from behind the viewing window as the surgeon, through a dissecting microscope, removed the outer covering of the eye. Next the four rectus muscles were detached from the eyeball, then the surgeon placed a hemostat on the stump of the last severed eye muscle. With special long, minimally curved scissors, he cut the optic nerve. Sam's battered heart sank, realizing the monumental change that single surgical incision had made to his son's vision. He stood motionless, unable to take in a breath, emotion flooding through his veins as next the surgeon removed the eyeball.

Unable to swallow the thickening lump in his throat, Sam watched as a nurse stood nearby with a small specimen container to collect a tiny piece of the optic nerve for histopathologic study. For their next huge hold-your-breath diagnosis—had all of the cancer been removed or had it spread? His stomach pinched at the potential outcome. The doctor worked painstakingly to also open the eye globe to harvest tissue from the retinoblastoma. Before closing, he placed a plastic temporary conformer into Dani's eye socket to avoid a shrunken look and maintain a natural shape. They'd discussed in advance how this would be done in preparation to ensure the proper size and motility for the future eye prosthesis.

When he finally could, Sam took a deep breath. The worst was over, no, check that, the worst had been getting the damn diagnosis of cancer in the first place. Since he wanted to keep a positive outlook, he'd deemed today the first step in Dani's healing. He watched like a hawk as the anesthesiologist prepared his son for transfer to the recovery room and the surgical nurse bandaged Dani's left eye with a special patch to help decrease swelling.

He rushed out of the observation deck and hustled down the stairs to be the first to talk with Dr. Van Diesel when he exited the OR.

"All went well," the white-haired man said, as he tossed his gloves in the trash and removed the surgical cap then the mask from his face. "No surprises." He forced a smile that looked more like a squint. "Should be a couple of days before we get the pathology reports."

"Thank you." And Sam probably wouldn't sleep until he knew whether the tumor had spread or not. But he was determined to keep that positive attitude. As of right now the tumor was gone, his son was free of cancer. That was how it had to be.

The doctor continued on to the locker room. Sam stood outside the OR doors and waited for the team to transport Dani. Several minutes later the doors swung open and his son, looking so tiny on the huge gurney, got rolled toward the recovery room.

He followed the medical parade out of the surgical suite, down the hall and into Recovery. As he was a staff member as well as a parent, he was also allowed to accompany the boy rather than be instructed to wait outside until he was ready for discharge. The receiving RR nurses bustled around the gurney, transferring him to their bed, disconnecting Dani from the OR equipment and attaching him to theirs. Heart monitor, blood-pressure cuff, pulse oximeter, oxygen.

Sam remained by his son's side, taking his tiny yet pudgy fingers into his own, feeling their chill and asking for a second blanket to cover him. Every once in a while his son moved or took a deeper breath. His heartbeat was steady and strong, blipping across the monitor screen; his blood pressure read low for a three-year-old, but he was still sedated. One particular Filipino nurse looked after Dani as if he were her own. That gave Sam reassurance.

"Is your wife coming, Doctor?" Her Filipino accent made the sentence staccato.

"No." Sam shook his head. "No wife."

He'd lost the woman with whom he'd thought he'd spend the rest of his life. She'd walked away. But he'd committed to adopting little Dani and he couldn't bear the thought of disappointing the boy who would finally have a home and a family of his own. Even if it was just the two of them.

"I will watch him," the nurse said. "Don't worry. You should take a break."

He stretched and glanced at her name tag. "Thank you, Imelda. I could use a cup of coffee about now."

She nodded toward the nurses' lunchroom. "We just made some."

He thought about taking her up on the offer but realized how much he needed to stretch his legs, to get his blood moving again. To help him think. To plan. Maybe with more circulation to his brain he'd be able to process everything that'd happened today. "Thanks, but I'm going to take a walk."

He stood and started to leave, then blurted the first thought in his mind. "By any chance, do you know where the prosthetic eye department is?"

Imelda pulled in her double chin. "Do we have one, Doctor?"

He tipped his head. Good question. Hadn't Dr. Van Diesel mentioned it at one point? "I hope so."

As he left the recovery room, he made eye contact with the charge nurse. "I'll be back in twenty minutes but beep me the instant Dani wakes up, okay?"

She nodded, so he pushed the metal plate on the wall and the recovery room department doors automatically swung inward. With one more glance over his shoulder to his sleeping son, and another pang in his heart, he stepped outside.

The one-hour operation under general anesthesia was fairly routine, and because the eye was surrounded by bone, it made it much easier for Dani to tolerate. If all went well, his son could even be discharged later that afternoon.

He walked down the hall, entered the elevator. His mind drifted to Katie, wondering if this pain would have been easier to take sharing it with someone else, but that was never to be. Katie had stuck with him all through medical school and his pediatric residency at UCLA while she'd tried to launch her acting career. Sure, they'd talked about marriage and children, but mostly he'd avoided it. He'd been left by the most important woman in his life, his mother, at a tender age, and it had marked him for life. Toward the end of their relationship, she'd kept insisting on wedding plans and he'd kept sidestepping them. When he'd finally brought up marriage because of the adoption, after screaming at him for making such a huge decision by himself Katie had suddenly decided her acting career needed her full attention.

He'd screwed up by not consulting her, but he'd thought he'd known her, and she'd very nearly wrenched his heart right out of his chest when she'd walked away.

Not a great track record with the women he'd loved. At least his foster mother, Mom Murphy, had never sent him back.

The elevator stopped at the first-floor lobby and he headed to the information desk. "Don't we have a department that makes facial prosthetics here? You know, things like eyes?"

The silver-haired gentleman's gaze lit with knowledge. "Yes, as a matter of fact, I believe we do." He scrolled through his computer directory, then used his index finger to point. "It's called Ocularistry and Anaplastology." The man had trouble pronouncing it and made a second attempt. "And it's in the basement, with Pathology." He placed his hand beside his mouth as if to whisper. "I think it's next door to the morgue."

"What's the name of the head of the department?" Sam asked.

"Judith Rimmer. Or, as we volunteers like to call her, Helen Mirren without the star power. Hubba-hubba, if you know what I mean."

Sam's brows rose at the thought—so even old guys had crushes—but off to the dungeon he went. Once he exited the elevator, he wondered why the fluorescent lights even looked dimmer down in the hospital basement, but pressed on. He passed the Matériel Management department, then Central Service—the cleaning and sterilization area. He knew where Pathology was—he'd visited there regularly to get early reports on his patients and to discuss prognoses with the pathologists. He'd also unfortunately been to the morgue far more often than he cared to in the line of duty. Nothing cut deeper than losing a child patient, and for the sake of science he'd sat in on his share of autopsies to help make sense of the tragedies.

Sam sidestepped the morgue double doors, refusing to even glance through the ocean-liner-style windows for activity, then squinted and saw the small department sign for Ocularistry and Anaplastology in bold black letters. How many people would even know what it meant?

The office was shoved into the farthest corner in the hallway, as if it had been an afterthought. The panel of fluorescent lights just outside the door blinked and buzzed, in need of a new tube, making things seem eerier than they already were. He wasn't sure whether to knock or just go inside. He glanced at his watch, he'd wasted enough time finding the department, so without a moment's further hesitation he pushed through the door of the "prosthetic eye people's" department.

A dainty, young platinum-blonde woman with short hair more in style with a 1920s flapper than current fashion arranged flesh-colored silicone ears under a glass display case, as if they were necklaces and earrings in an upscale jewelry store. She looked nothing like Helen Mirren but might pass as her granddaughter. What had that volunteer been talking about? On the next table sat a huge model of an eyeball. He narrowed his gaze at the odd juxtaposition.

The woman glanced up with warm brown eyes surrounded with dark liner and smoky underlid smudges. Not the usual look he noticed in the hospital, and the immediate draw caught him off guard. His son was in Recovery, having just lost an eye, for God's sake. He had no right to notice an attractive woman! The fact he did ticked him off.

"I'm looking for Judith Rimmer." Okay, so he sounded gruffer than necessary, maybe impatient, but it wasn't even noon and he'd already been through one hell of a no-good, very bad day, to paraphrase one of his son's favorite books.

"She's currently in Europe," Andrea Rimmer said. The intruder had barged in and brought a whole lot of stress with him, and her immediate response was to bristle.

The brown-haired man with intense blue eyes, of which neither was prosthetic, stared her down, not liking her answer one bit. He may be a head taller than she was, but she wasn't about to let him intimidate her. She'd had plenty of practice of standing up to men like that with her father.

"When will she be back?" He seemed to look right through her, which further ticked her off. Wasn't she a person, too? Was her grandmother the only one who mattered in this department?

"Next week." She could play vague with the best of them.

"I'll come back then."

It hadn't been her idea to take the apprenticeship for ocularist four years ago. Nope, that had been good old Dad's plan. She'd barely graduated from the Los Angeles Art Academy when he'd pressured her into getting a "real job" while she found her bearings in the art world. Now that she was in her last year of the apprenticeship, and since Grandma was threatening to retire and was expecting Andrea to take her place, she'd felt her back against the wall and resented the narrow choice being shoved down her throat. Work full-time. Run the department. The place didn't even have windows!

What about her painting? Her dreams?

Had the demanding doctor brushed her off by assuming she was an inexperienced technician because she was young? She didn't think twenty-eight was that young, but being short probably made her seem younger. If he thought he could be rude because she was young or a nobody, this guy with the tense attitude had just pushed her intolerant button.

"She may not *be* coming back." She sounded snotty, which wasn't her usual style, as she rearranged the ears again. But she didn't really care because this guy, who may be good-looking but seriously lacked the charm gene so who cared how good-looking he was, had just ruined her morning for no good reason.

She glanced up. He raised a brow and stared her down

in response to her borderline impudent reply, and she saw the judgment there, the same look she'd seen in her father's eyes time and time again. *I'm a doctor. You dare to talk to me like that?*

The imaginary conversation quickly played out in her head. *What? Am I not good enough for you?* A feeling, unfortunately, she'd had some experience with on the home front most of her life. After all, wasn't she the daughter of a woman with only a high-school education? A stay-at-home mother keeping a spotless house for a husband who rarely visited? A woman so depressed she'd turned into a shadow of her former self? Half of her DNA might be genius, but the other half, often insinuated by her father, was suspect. Well, good ol' Dad should have thought about that before knocking up her mother if it meant so damn much to him.

The invading doctor continued to stare down his nose at her. Andrea wasn't about to back down now. The nerve. Did he think she was a shopgirl, a department receptionist minding the store while Granny frolicked in France? She'd just spent a week making this latest batch of silicone ears, measuring the patients to perfection, matching the skin color, creating the simplest and most secure way to adhere them to what was left of their own ears. And unless anyone looked really closely, no one would notice. Just ask the struggling musician Brendan, who'd had his earlobe chopped off by a mobster, what he thought about her skills!

"What do you mean, she may not be coming back?" His tone shifted to accusing as if he should have been privy to the memo and voted on the decision. Wasn't that how demanding doctors, just like her father, behaved? *I need this* now. *Don't annoy me with facts.* He stood, hands on hips, his suit jacket pushed aside, revealing his trim and flat stomach—wait, she didn't care about his physique because he was rude—refusing to look away from the visual contact they'd made. Something really had this guy bothered, and she was the unfortunate party getting the brunt of it.

"It's called retirement."

His wild blue stare didn't waver, and, as illogical as it seemed under the circumstances, something was going on with the electrical charge circulating around her skin because of him.

A beeper went off on his belt, breaking the standoff and the static tickling across her arms. He glanced at it. She was glad because she really didn't know how much longer she could take him standing in the small outer office, and most especially gazing into those intense eyes.

It was her job to notice things like that. Eyes. Yeah, she'd become quite an expert during her apprenticeship. If she kept telling herself that, maybe she wouldn't scold herself later for falling under the spell of a completely pompous stranger based solely on his baby blues.

"I've gotta go." Obviously in no mood to deal with her touchy technician act, he turned and huffed off, right out the door.

Wilting over her bad behavior, she tossed her pen onto the countertop and plopped into the nearest chair. Why had she behaved that way with him? She'd knee-jerked over the intruding and demanding doctor, but wasn't he acting exactly like her father? Arrogant and overbearing. Lording his station in life over her. *Where's the head of the department, because you're not good enough. Step out of my way.* He didn't need to say the words; she'd *felt* them.

Andrea caught herself making a lemon-sucking expression and let it go. Maybe she was the one with the attitude, and she hadn't even tried to control it. That man had just got the brunt of it, too. Truth was, she needed to be more accommodating to clients and doctors, especially if she actually ever agreed to take over as the department head.

Which she sure as heck wasn't certain she wanted to do. Especially if catering to demanding doctors like that guy would be part of the routine.

She hadn't expected a young doctor with such interestingly pigmented irises—because that was what she'd learned to notice since beginning her apprenticeship—and penetrating eyes as that guy's to set her off on a rant. And she'd acted nothing short of an ass with him.

Shame on her.

Guilt and longing intertwined inside her. She'd fallen short of the mark just now, and it was a symptom of the battle she fought every day when she came to work. This was her job, creating prosthetic eyes for people who needed them, silicone ears, noses and cheeks for cancer victims and veterans, too, and it was a noble profession. She actually loved it. Loved the patients and making their lives better. But she liked things the way they were— working four days a week at the hospital and painting the other three. Her heart yearned to paint, not run a windowless department in the bowels of a hospital.

Andrea put her elbows on the counter and rested her forehead in the palms of her hands. If Grandma ever retired, some lousy department head *she* would make.

A week later...

It had taken Sam a good day and a half to calm down after his ridiculous encounter with the young woman in the O&A department. Where did they find the employees these days anyway? But to be fair, she didn't have a clue that he'd just come from watching his son have his eye removed in surgery. He may have been more demanding than usual, but he'd been in no shape to judge how he'd come off to her, or, at that moment, to care. All he'd wanted had been to ensure his boy could have the best person possible make a realistic-looking eye to replace the one Dani had lost.

That woman couldn't have been more than in her early twenties. How could she possibly have the skill...? Yet, he reminded himself, he'd eventually realized that Judith Rimmer had a reputation known all over the country for excellence in her specialty. He'd read up on her online while little Dani had napped one afternoon. She wouldn't leave her beloved department in the hands of a novice. Would she?

Now, having completely calmed down, and being back on the job with a miraculous break in his schedule that morning, thanks to a no-show patient, Sam prepared to return to the basement to discuss Dani's need for an eye.

He reached the ocularistry and anaplastology department door, took a deep breath and entered with a plan to apologize for inadvertently insulting the still-wet-behind-the-ears ocularist—if that was even what she was. How could he know for sure? They hadn't gotten that far. Because his foster mother hadn't raised an ungracious son—she'd knock him upside the head from the grave if she found out, too. Nor had she raised a son to judge a book by the young cover—not with the revolving door of foster kids with whom he'd grown up. He smiled inwardly, then swung open the door, and much to his surprise found Helen Mirren's double, not retired but standing right in front of him beside a row of unblinking eyeballs in all colors in a display case. She wore something that looked like a sun visor but with magnifying glasses attached and a headlight, examining one specific eye as if it were a huge diamond.

Sitting with an expectant gaze on her face was the girl, who, on second encounter, and with all that eye makeup, looked more like the iconic 1960s model from Great Britain. Twiggy, was it? But not nearly as skinny. This girl had curves. She obviously waited for Judith's approval on something, a project she'd made? Maybe, but, no matter what the scene was about, Sam was ticked off. Again.

The young woman finally noticed someone had entered and glanced at him, a quick look of surprise in her double take. Yeah, he'd caught her in a childish lie, so he glared back. He could act as juvenile as the next person, thanks to his four older foster brothers and two younger foster sisters, countless other foster siblings constantly coming through the family revolving door and foster parents who hadn't been afraid to make threats in order to tame the often out-of-control tribe.

"Reconsidering retirement, Ms. Rimmer?" His vision drifted to a perplexed Judith.

Judith's gaze flitted back and forth between the woman and Sam, obviously trying to figure out what their history had been.

"Technically I wasn't lying, because my grandmother plans to retire as soon as I'm ready and *willing* to take over." She stood, which hardly made a difference. What was she, five feet, tops? And jumped right in with an explanation. "And, for all I knew, she could've been swept away by the beauty of Europe and decided not to come home. To retire on the spot. It could've happened."

Her outlandish cover nearly made him smile. Nearly. But he held firm because he found himself enjoying her flushed cheeks and her mildly flaring nostrils as she explained, her raccoon-painted eyes taking on more of a fawn-ready-to-bolt appearance.

"Which makes it okay that you lied to me?" He wasn't ready to let her off the hook, though.

She stepped around the counter, taking two steps toward him, never breaking the visual connection, which was surprisingly stimulating. "You came in with a nasty attitude that day and proceeded to make me feel like a novice who couldn't possibly be of help to you. So I decided not to be any help at all."

So that's how she'd read him. For a second he felt like a chump, but she deserved the full story. An explanation for why he'd been that jerk. "I'd just come from watching my son's enucleation. I needed reassurance he could look normal again."

Her challenging expression instantly melted into an apologetic peacemaking plea. "Oh." Those huge eyes immediately watered. "I'm so sorry to hear that."

"Dr.—" Judith read his name badge "—Marcus, I'm sorry the two of you got off to a rocky start, I'm also very sorry about your son, but I assure you Andrea is as skilled as they come. And because I'm completely booked up with projects, having just returned from vacation, she'd be happy to help you with your son's eye prosthesis. I assure you, with her artistic background, she'll make a perfect match and fit."

Andrea sent a quick questioning glance toward her grandmother but immediately recovered, as if she'd gotten the clear message to play along. *Was* she a novice? Sam still wasn't convinced. She looked so young.

"So, what I'll need to do—" Andrea used an index finger to lightly scratch the corner of her mouth "—is make an appointment for you to bring in your son. Is he completely healed yet? We shouldn't take measurements until he is."

"It's only been a week, but he's doing really well."

"Let's make it next week, then, to be safe. I'll need to take photos of his other eye and make a silicone cast of his healed eye socket. After that I'll make a wax version, which I'll be able to mold as needed to fit. What's your son's name?"

"Danilo, but he goes by Dani."

She nodded, sincerity oozing out of those huge brown

eyes. "What day is good for you?" She brought up a calendar on the computer—back to business—and he fished out his pocket phone, tapping through to his work calendar.

Back and forth they went, politely trying to work out an appointment day and time. His schedule was overbooked, since he'd taken off a week to be with his son after the surgery, which was why he was aggravated that one of his patients was a no-show today and would need to be rescheduled, further keeping him backed up. Yet that was the only reason he'd been able to sneak down here at this moment, which had turned out to be a good thing. Which would all be beside the point if he couldn't make an appointment.

At least for now, since his return to work, his former foster sister Cat could be Dani's caregiver during the day. She lived within five miles of him and was a stay-at-home mom who needed the extra cash. Their arrangement worked out for everyone, since she also had two children under the age of five, and Dani loved to play with the other kids. He scratched his head, at a loss.

Why hadn't he considered his work issue when he'd known Dani would need the prosthetic eye right off? The bigger question was why hadn't he considered how difficult it would be to become a single father in the first place?

Of course, that hadn't been his original plan…

Yeah, he was in over his head, but it made no difference, because he was proud and happy to be Dani's father, no matter how hard and complicated life had become because of it. Add another point to foster Mom's tally, *the kid needed a home*. "Do you do house calls, by any chance?"

Andrea dipped her head, thinking for a second. "No. But since I gave you a hard time last week, I'll make an exception for you, Dr. Marcus."

All was forgiven. Sweet brown-eyed angel from

heaven. "Call me Sam, please," he said, on a rush of relief. "I really appreciate that."

Their earlier glowering contest faded to a distant memory when she smiled at him. It was more of a Mona Lisa
smile, but it drew his attention to her mouth and he noticed a pair of classic lips with the delicate twin peaks of
a Cupid's bow.

"So how about this day next week, at your house, say,
sevenish?"

"Sounds like a plan, Ms....?"

"Rimmer, but please call me Andrea."

"Are you related to Dr. Rimmer?" The tyrant of Cardiac Surgery?

"Yes. Andrea's my granddaughter," Judith spoke up,
reminding Sam that Dr. Rimmer was her son. Why he
hadn't made the connection earlier was beyond him.

"I hope you won't hold that against me," Andrea said
drily, as though reading his thoughts and bearing the
weight of her father's perilous reputation. She glanced
sheepishly at her grandmother, a good sign that Andrea
cared about her and didn't want to insult her son, though
it seemed clear she knew what Sam's surprised reaction
had been about.

Since they'd skimmed over last week's argument and
had moved on to peace talks, he wouldn't bring up his
multiple grievances about the curmudgeon cardiac surgery department head who wanted to throw his weight
around the entire hospital. Instead he dug deep into his
bag of tricks and pulled out a smile. Admittedly, since his
breakup with Katie, and Dani's diagnosis, he'd nearly forgotten how, but seeing Andrea's immediate relieved reaction, her expression brightening and those lovely lips
parting into a grin, he was glad he had. Plus he'd meant
that smile and it felt pretty damn good.

Because she was the first lady to get him riled up in ages, and he liked how that jacked up his ticker. She'd made him feel nearly human again.

"Next Tuesday, then. Seven. It's a date, Andrea."

CHAPTER TWO

ANDREA TAPPED ON the white front door of the boxy mid-century modern home in the hills above Glendale. She was about to ring the bell when the door swung open. Admittedly nervous about facing the handsome Dr. Sam Marcus on his turf, she grinned tensely until she saw him with an adorable little boy balanced on his hip and wearing an eye patch, then she relaxed.

"Come in," he said, seeming more hospitable than she would have imagined considering their first two encounters.

"Hi," she said, stepping inside onto expensive-looking white tile in the narrow entryway. "This must be Dani." She moved closer to the little boy, raised her brows and gave a closed-mouth smile. He buried his face in his father's shoulder. *Ack, too much.*

"Bashful," Sam mouthed.

She nodded and pretended to ignore the adorable little person after that, as Sam bypassed the living room and walked her into the more inviting family room. It was large, square, open and with excellent sources of natural light from tall windows nearly covering one entire wall of the boxy '50s architecture. As it was late April, the sun stuck around longer and longer, and though his house abutted mixed-tree-covered hills and stood on metal stilts at the front, the angle at this time of day was perfect for maximum light. A thick brown carpet made her want to kick off her shoes and walk barefoot. Not sure what to do next, she set her backpack and art box aka fishing-tackle box on the classic stone fireplace hearth, then glanced up at Sam. The previously upturned corners of his mouth had stretched into a genuine smile.

She'd given herself a stern talking-to the afternoon they'd made the appointment for letting herself send and pick up on some kind of natural attraction vibes arcing between them. The man was a father! Probably married. How many do-overs would she need with this guy?

Shifting her gaze from Sam, she secretly studied Dani so as not to send him into ostrich mode again. She was admittedly surprised that Dani wasn't a mini-me of Sam. He looked Asian, Filipino maybe? Was he adopted? And Sam didn't wear a wedding ring, which made her wonder if he might not be married, but she figured she'd find out soon enough once his wife or significant other made an appearance.

"That's as good a place as any to set up," he said, easing Dani down onto his own two feet. "I hope the lighting is good enough."

"This should be perfect."

Dani immediately ran toward his stack of toys.

"Um, should I wait for your wife?"

"I'm not married. I adopted Dani on my own." Sam sat on the large wraparound couch and put his feet up on the circular ottoman at the center.

"That's fantastic." *Don't sound so enthusiastic!* "The adoption part, I mean." The only men she knew in Los Angeles who adopted kids on their own were gay. Dr. Marcus clearly didn't fall into that category if she read that subtle humming interest between them right.

"I knew what you meant." A kind gaze came winging

her way, and she felt her anxiety over making a dumb remark take a step down.

"Does he speak English?"

"They spoke both English and Tagalog at the orphanage. He's superbright and picks up more and more words every day." Spoken like a proud papa.

She found the boy busy with a colorful toy TV controller, punching buttons and listening to sounds and jingles, and dropped to her knees. "So, Dani, may I look under your patch?"

The black-haired toddler, who was small for his age, kept his head down, staring at the gadget in his hand, as he let her gingerly remove the child-sized patch. She'd seen empty eye socket after empty eye socket in the four years since she'd started the apprenticeship, but this was her first toddler. Grandma had given her a pep talk that afternoon about how much she believed in Andrea's talent and technical skills, and truth was she knew she'd caught on quickly to the long and tedious process of re-creating matching eyes for the eyeless. But this was a beautiful little kid, and her heart squeezed every time she looked at him, thinking this was way too early for anyone to need a prosthetic. But was there ever a good age?

She'd worn stretch slacks, so she sat cross-legged beside him in order to be at his level. "I need to make a little cast to fit your face, Dani. Will you let me do that?"

The boy looked at his father, who reassured him it was okay with a slow, deep nod.

"It won't hurt, I promise, but it might feel strange and cold for a little while." With adult patients it was so much easier to explain the process. She'd just have to wing it with Dani. "May I take some pictures of your eye, too?"

"Eye gone," he said, slapping his palm over the left socket, as if she didn't know.

"This eye." She pointed to the right one.

"Okay." She could hardly hear him.

"Thank you." She blinked when he glanced up. "Do you ever play with clay?"

He nodded shyly.

"This stuff is kind of like clay. Want to watch?"

"Okay."

"Here, you can touch it."

He did but immediately pulled back his hand at the feel of the foreign, gooey substance.

Andrea worked quickly to make enough casting gel to press into the empty socket area, and when it was time, Sam held Dani's head still while she gently pressed it into the completely healed cavity. "Cold?"

"Uh-huh."

"But it doesn't hurt, right?"

He shook his head and they smiled at each other. He understood she hadn't lied. A sudden urge to cuddle the boy had her skimming her clean palm across his short-cropped hair instead. "How'd you get to be so sweet?"

"Don't know."

A surge of emotion made her eyes prickle. This precious guy had already lost an eye to cancer. How was that for a huge dose of reality to a toddler? She swallowed against the moisture gathering in her throat. "I bet you were born sweet." Was this how it felt to flirt with a little kid?

The statement wasn't the least bit funny, but Dani thought it was and he giggled, his remaining almond-shaped eye almost closing when he did. She hadn't been around many children since way back when she used to babysit for movie money, but something about Dani made her want to kiss his chubby cheeks and touch the tip of his rounded nose with her pointer finger.

She wiped her hands clean and dug out her camera from the backpack. "May I take your picture?"

"Uh-huh." He watched her as if mesmerized, but also maybe a little afraid to move with the cast in place and taking form.

"I have to get really close to your eye. Is that okay?"

"Yes."

She leaned in toward his cute out-sticking ear and whispered, "I promise not to touch your eye, just take pictures."

He sat perfectly still and stared at her camera as she focused and zoomed in and shot photo after photograph of his dark brown orb. Later she'd study that eye until she had it memorized, then, and only then, would she attempt the intricate painting of his iris. Making eyes was a long and tedious process that took anywhere between sixteen and occasionally up to eighty hours, even though there was a big push to go digital these days. Mistakes weren't acceptable in Grandma's world. Neither was digital technology. Andrea had learned early on to take the extra time and effort at the beginning to save hours of do-overs. And she loved that part of her job.

By the age of three she knew the human eye was just a hair smaller by one or two millimeters than it would eventually become, and that by the age of thirteen it would reach the full adult size. Danilo would probably need a new prosthesis at that time, if not before, but she planned to make this one to last a full decade. The boy deserved no less.

After four minutes the timer went off, alerting her that the silicone was set. Tomorrow, back in the O&A department, she'd duplicate it in wax and later reform it until it fit Dani perfectly, which would give her another excuse to see the adorable little guy. There'd be multiple reasons to see Dani, since he'd have a trial period of wearing a clear acrylic beneath his patch for fitting purposes for the next month while she re-created his iris.

"I'm all done. What do you think about that?" She

gently eased out the silicone cast from his eye socket, brow line and upper cheek.

"Okay."

"And it didn't hurt, did it?"

He shook his head. She showed him what the cast looked like and he made a funny face, which made her laugh, then she carefully put the partial facial and eye-socket cast into a protective carrying case. Dani watched every move she made, as if she might be taking part of his face with her. She handed him a mirror to see she'd left all of him behind. He stoically studied himself, missing eye and all, which made her want to brighten him up.

Andrea raised her brows and pressed her lips together before talking. "Did you know I brought you a present?"

His other eye widened. "No." So serious.

"I brought you my favorite stuffed frog." She reached into her backpack and pulled out the bean-stuffed toy that used to sit on her computer monitor at work. She'd grabbed it on a whim just before she'd left tonight. "His name is Ribbit."

Dani giggled again. "I like him."

"Here. He's yours. You earned him for being so good." She offered him the toy, and he reached for it without hesitation.

"What do you say?" For the first time in the entire process Sam spoke up.

"Thank you."

She couldn't help herself and kissed his forehead. "You are welcome."

Sam cleared his throat. "Can I make you some tea or coffee?"

"Tea sounds good. Thanks." There was a strange expression in Sam's eyes when theirs met, as if maybe he'd been touched by the interchange with her and Dani as much as she had.

Dani played happily with his frog as Andrea helped put the eye patch back on. "There. Now you look like a pirate."

"I don't like pirate."

"When I make your new eye, you won't need to wear the patch anymore."

He touched the patch and tugged on it. "Okay."

"Hey, is this your truck?" She crawled over to a pile of toys in the corner of the room. "May I play with it?" The boy quickly followed her and laughed when she made a vroom-vroom sound, pushing the red truck around the carpet, while waiting for Sam to make the tea.

Next they played building blocks, and Dani took great pleasure in letting her build her colorful tower, only to knock it down the instant she'd finished. She pretended to be upset, folding her arms and pouting, but the boy saw right through her. Mostly what they did was laugh, giggle, tease each other and horse around until Sam showed up with the tea.

"I hate to break up the play, Dani, but it's time to get you ready for bed."

Dani acted upset. He pushed out his lower lip and crossed his chubby arms just like Andrea had done a few moments before, but she knew it was all a show. He'd been rubbing his right eye when they'd played, like any little kid who was getting sleepy. When he thought she wasn't looking, he'd even yawned.

"Oh, jammies," Andrea said, to distract him from his pout. "I bet you've got really cool jammies."

"My jammies have trucks," he said, his sweet single-eyed gaze waiting for her reaction.

"Trucks! I think you already know how much I love trucks."

She was positive she saw him puff out his chest. Sam offered his hand and Dani took it, looking happily up at his father. The moment went still in her mind like a photograph, as she admired the sweet boy with the loving new parent he'd had the good fortune to find. But before he left the room she called after him. "Dani, don't forget your frog."

He trotted back to take it and gave her one last smile before running off to his father's waiting hand, then walking with him down the hall. Andrea sat on the plush carpet and sipped her fragrant chamomile tea, her heart aching for a precious little boy with one eye. The warm tea helped smooth out the lump in her throat, but there was no way she'd soon forget Dani.

A large framed black-and-white photograph on the opposite wall caught her attention. She carried her tea over to it and counted eight kids with a mother and father, all grinning, on someone's front lawn. She studied the enlarged grainy family photo and determined that the boy third from the end might possibly be Sam Marcus. Or maybe he was second in? Come to think of it, there wasn't a very strong family resemblance.

A tallish woman with a broad smile and clear-looking eyes stood next to a droopy-shouldered man with a soft, kind face. They both had dark hair. Two of the kids looked even less like the rest, a blonde girl and a gangly boy with a buzz cut, but somehow those two had earned the favored position of each standing under a draping arm of the mother. Maybe that was Sam under her right arm? Who knew? The date at the bottom of the blown-up picture read "1990." That would make Dr. Marcus somewhere around thirty.

Andrea's gaze wandered to another wall and a shiny silver frame with beautiful cursive penmanship on a weathered scroll inside. The title read "Legend of the Starfish" and the short allegory taught that though a person might not be able to save everyone, in this case starfish, they could at least help one at a time. She stood pondering the words, sipping her tea, wondering what this told her about Dr. Samuel Marcus, the single guy who'd adopted a little boy from the Philippines.

Ten minutes had passed. She'd put all of Dani's toys back where they belonged and had almost finished her herbal tea when Sam returned. He wore comfortable jeans that still managed to hug his hips and thighs, and a white with black stripes polo shirt he hadn't bothered to tuck in. It gave her a glimpse of his broader-than-she'd-expected chest and surprising biceps. He walked around in his socks, proving he was totally at home in his castle. His cell phone rang. He checked the caller and said, "Sorry, but I've got to take this. It's my sister." She nodded her approval.

"You're up late," he said, then walked around the room in brief yet very familiar conversation. She tried not to listen, though envying him having a sister to share things with.

His hair was less tidy tonight, and Andrea liked the effect, especially when a clump fell forward onto his forehead when he bent over to pick up an overlooked toy block. And the eyes that had practically drilled a hole into her the last time they'd met seemed smoky blue tonight without a trace of tension around them. She'd often heard the term "boyish good looks," but never understood what that meant until now. How could that uptight man who'd barged into her department be the same guy standing in front of her? A man who'd adopted a little boy on his own and appeared to genuinely enjoy a conversation with his sister. A man like that had to have a good heart.

She took in a tiny breath as he ended the call and approached, her enjoying every step. So this was what an everyday hero looked like. Feeling nothing short of smitten, she let out a beyond-friendly smile.

Sam didn't know why he'd choked up just before he'd

put Dani to bed, but seeing Andrea with his son, and how effortlessly they'd gotten along, made him remember how much Katie had let him down. Evidently having her own kids would have been one thing, but it'd been too much for her to consider adopting someone else's child. "You never know what you'll get," she'd said. "You could be adopting a million problems." He'd argued that the same could be said for any child. Besides, he'd seen with his own eyes what wonders selfless understanding and generosity of love could work on most kids. His foster mother had been the queen of that, not only with her own children but with all the kids she'd brought into their home.

He wasn't about to go down Katie's road of disappointment and pain again, especially right now, not when the dramatic-looking, height-challenged blonde with big overly made-up brown eyes sat waiting for him. He smiled and she gave a flirtatious beam right back. He definitely liked that, even though he knew a smile like that could be dangerous.

"You've made quite an impression. Dani said to tell you good-night."

"Great. He's an awfully sweet kid."

"Yeah, he has a gentle nature." Now wasn't the time to go all soft over the misfortune of his beautiful adopted son, and how sometimes it reminded him of his own situation as a child, so he focused on his tea. "My tea's gone cold. Can I refill yours?" He scooped up his cup and took hers when she offered it to him, then headed for the kitchen. Surprisingly, she followed along in her bare feet. He liked it that she'd made herself at home.

He put their cups on the kitchen counter, and as he turned on the front burner to heat the teapot, he felt her expectant gaze. He glanced over his shoulder and found her still smiling at him, so he smiled back, letting her warmth pass through him. If they kept up this goofy grinning, things could get awkward.

"It's really obvious you're a good and loving father."

"I don't know how true that is, but he deserves no less." He kept busy, opening and closing drawers and cabinets, but talked freely.

Something about her easygoing and encouraging style helped him open up. "You know my greatest fear is that Dani might lose his other eye. They say the odds are low with a single retinoblastoma, but having gone through this with him I guess I'm still afraid it could happen again. And the kid so doesn't deserve any of this." He bit back his frustration.

Andrea kept quiet, cuing him to keep talking, so he did. "No matter what happens, my goal is to make as normal a life as possible for Dani."

"I can tell how much you care about him." She folded her hands on the quartz surface, and he thought the counter was high for her stature. She'd need a little stool to wash dishes at this sink. The thought tickled him and made the corner of his mouth quirk, imagining her standing on a stool in his kitchen, washing plates. So domestic, so different than the artistic impression she gave. Where had that thought come from?

She couldn't be more than five feet, but what a powerhouse. She'd probably never be caught dead washing dishes for a guy. He sensed she'd never let anyone take advantage of her. She sure as hell hadn't let him that day. Thinking back to her stern father, he was sure she'd probably had to grow a steel spine to survive. Yeah, no way she'd be a happy dishwasher.

He poured them both more tea and they sat at the kitchen table, and because she was so easy to be around, and seemed so sympathetic toward Dani, he decided to really open up. "I'm afraid people will look at Dani and pity him, which, by the way, you absolutely didn't do. Thanks for that."

She dipped her head and blinked slowly, then took a sip of her tea, so serious. "I've had a lot of practice with our clientele."

"I'm sure you have." He sipped, but the tea was too hot, so he put the cup on the table. "I also worry that other kids will be curious about his fake eye and make him self-conscious."

"I think all kids are self-conscious about something."

A quick flash of him being around seven or eight and having to wear faded thrift-store shirts that didn't fit to school, because that was all his mother could afford, reminded him firsthand about self-consciousness.

"The thing is, I don't want him to slip into the mindset of feeling inferior. That could set the tone for the rest of his life. I'd hate for that to happen." He'd been fighting those feelings his entire life, and he'd obviously said something to move Andrea, because she leaned forward and her hand cupped his forearm and tightened.

"I'm going to make the most perfect eye ever for him. The other kids won't even notice."

"Then it'll be my job to teach him to be totally independent, not afraid to try things." His crazy, lovable foster family came to mind. "Hell, if he takes after any of his new uncles, he'll give me gray hair before my time."

"I think your plan is perfect. Dani's a lucky boy to have you as his father. By the way, is that your family in that big picture?"

He considered the Murphys his family, especially after he'd been taken away from his mother at ten and she'd officially given him up when he'd been twelve—which had hurt like nothing he'd ever experienced before and could never be matched until Katie had walked away—

and they'd kept him until he'd been eighteen, then sent him off to college.

"Yep. The big clan, circa 1990. I was around ten in that one."

"Ah, you were the middle brother. I thought I recognized you." She laughed lightly, and he was glad she'd taken the time to look at his family picture, but didn't feel like going into the complicated explanation of who they really were. He hardly knew her. He'd let her think what he let the rest of the world think—he'd come from a big, happy family.

"Yeah, try being in the middle of four daredevil brothers. Those guys were tough acts to follow. Probably why I went into medicine." His professional choice had also been part of his determination to prove the positive impact fostering could have. It had been his way of giving something back. But she didn't need to know that, either.

She smiled and he grinned back. He found his smiles coming more often and easier, spending time with her. It felt good.

"I can only imagine." She went quiet.

They sat in silence for a while, him in deep thought about the responsibilities of being a single father, about how his parents had taught by example the importance of routine and stability in every kid's life, and having no clue what Andrea was ruminating about. Soon the tea was gone and she stood.

"Time to go?" How could he blame her? He'd gone quiet after the topic of his family had come up, then had gotten all maudlin about his lack of parental skills. Great company. Who'd want to stick around for more of that?

"Yes. I want to get an early start on my project tomorrow."

He stood now, too. "I'm really glad you're doing it."

"Really?"

"Yeah, you're not nearly as bad as I originally thought." They laughed together, and it lightened the shifting mood. He wanted that earlier ease back between them.

"Oh, yes, the impertinent ocularist strikes again," she teased. "But I could have sworn you started it."

"I was uptight. Give me a break."

He could tell from the benign look on her face that she *was* indeed giving him a break, that she totally understood, especially now having met Dani, and he truly appreciated that.

They headed for the family room, where her tackle box and backpack had been left, Dani's silicone cast safely tucked inside. "And I had no idea what you'd just been through." With the backpack over one shoulder she faced him, an earnest expression softening her serious face. "Please forgive me for being rude to you that day."

"I've already forgotten. Besides, after the way you and Dani became fast friends tonight, I kind of have to."

That got another smile and a breath of a laugh out of her.

He walked her to the door and allowed one quick thought about how great she looked in those black slacks and the pale blue sweater hugging her curves. It was so much better than those faded scrubs and that frumpy white lab coat.

They said good-night, and he asked when he'd need to bring Dani in for reshaping of the wax mold she planned to make.

"I'll be in touch," she said, "as soon as possible, I promise."

"Then I'll take you at your word."

They said their goodbyes. He closed the door and scratched his chin and let his mind wonder about the possibility of something more working out between him and the perky ocularist. That was a first since Katie, too, and a good thing. Wasn't it about time to start dating again? For an instant he realized how single mothers must feel, wondering if a man wanted to get involved with a lady with kids. Was that how it worked the other way around? Would it matter to Andrea, as it had mattered to Katie, that he was an adoptive father?

CHAPTER THREE

SAM STROLLED INTO the hospital employee cafeteria to grab a quick lunch before his afternoon clinic. He'd barely finished playing catch-up with his electronic charting and had about twenty minutes to spare. Going through the line, he grabbed the fish of the day, and his guess was as good as any as to what type of white fish it was. He went for the least overcooked vegetables, green beans, grabbed a whole wheat roll and a tossed green salad and was good to go.

After paying, he juggled his cafeteria tray and searched around the noisy and crowded room—which smelled entirely too much of garlic—for a place to sit. A pleasant surprise awaited him when he spotted the light blond hair of his new favorite ocularist, especially after the slam-dunk impression she'd made on Dani last night, and he made a straight line to where she sat. Fortunately, she was eating alone. And reading a book, so she didn't notice him coming.

"Is this seat taken?"

Andrea glanced up, totally distracted by whatever novel she'd been reading. "Oh, hi." An instant flash of recognition and a welcoming smile made him think he'd made the right decision. "No, join me."

"Thanks." The invitation, which he'd clearly forced, still managed to make him happy. He sat, but not before removing the dishes from his tray and balancing that against the leg of the table. From this angle he could see the book was a biography on the artist Jackson Pollock. "Reading picture books, I see. No wonder you and Dani got along so well." He could always manage superficial conversations easily enough, had learned early on it was a survival technique in the foster care system, which had been pointed out to him by his "mom" when he'd tried the old you-can't-reach-me routine at first. The quiet and withdrawn kids got moved around more than the ones who knew how to socialize. All he wanted to do was prove he was worth keeping. That was the truth.

She rolled her eyes at his awful attempt at humor. "America's cowboy artist. Our very own van Gogh, torment and all." She closed the book and gave all of her attention to him. He liked that. Her naturally beautiful eyes were less distracted by makeup today, which he definitely also liked.

"How's our project going?" He pushed around the green beans rather than taking a bite, then decided to pile them on top of the piece of fish, thinking it might help the bland cafeteria food have a little more flavor that way.

"I'm off to a good start. I'll need to see Dani again, though, to exactly fit the wax mold."

"I can have my sister bring him by this afternoon, if you'd like." Yeah, piling the food together hadn't helped enhance the flavor at all, but watching Andrea, hearing her voice, made the taste far more palatable. Next he dug into his salad.

"I should be able to work that in. Can she bring him around two-thirty?"

"I'll see." He got out his mobile phone and texted Cat, his foster sister, the one he felt closest to. Being a mother of two toddlers herself, plus the fact she lived five miles from him, it'd made sense to ask her to be his child-care provider when his parental leave came to an end and he had to go back to work. Not to mention the fact that her husband, Buddy, a welder, had agreed to her staying at home with their kids. They lived on a tight budget, and she could use the extra income that watching Dani brought. The way he saw it, it was a win-win situation.

Andrea took a dainty bite of her salad, and he smiled at her, then tore into his roll, slathering it with butter, then taking a bite. "So, do you eat here every day?"

"Not usually, but I came in early today to start Dani's mold and forgot to pack a lunch."

"Thanks for that." He got a return on his text. "She'll be here. Now I'll have to explain that you're located in the dungeon next to the ghoulish morgue." He finished his text and looked up to see her studying him. Had he been insensitive about her department and its location? Had he insinuated that hers was an inferior department? Hell, it didn't even have windows, even when right at this moment in time it was the most important department in the whole hospital for him and his son. "I'm sorry if that sounded mean. I have jerk tendencies. I blame it totally on the influence of four brothers."

"You do have a big family, I can't argue with that."

"Crazy big, but it made me who I am. Major flaws and all." He grinned at her and really liked what she returned. "Sorry." If he'd offended her about her department being in no man's land, she'd easily forgiven him, judging by the sweet smile that highlighted those gorgeous lips. He allowed himself a moment or two to check them out. And when was the last time he'd gotten carried away with wild ideas by a woman's mouth?

He took another bite of his food to distract him from thinking of what it would feel like to kiss her. "This has got to be the worst lunch I've had in a long time," he said, to cover his real thoughts. *But thanks for that luscious mouth of yours.*

"The salad's not bad."

He pushed his plate aside and pulled the salad bowl closer, deciding to take her up on her tip and stick with that and the roll. "Right about now I'm dreaming about Thai food."

"I love Thai food." She matched him bite for bite with the salad.

"Yeah? You like pineapple fried rice? Pad Thai?"

"Love it, and satay, peanut sauce, all of it."

"But have you ever had coconut curry with braised chicken and egg noodles?"

"No, and now my mouth is watering, thank you very much." She played with her salad, no longer taking bites.

"Sorry. Didn't mean to ruin your lunch, but sometime I'm going to have to take you to Hollywood Boulevard for my new favorite dish."

She tossed him a questioning glance over the vague remark. And, yes, he was testing the water. Playing it safe was a knack he'd developed, and always preferable to getting rejected.

"Uh, yes, I guess theoretically that was an invitation. You interested?"

"Well, you can't very well dangle coconut curry in front of me like that without inviting me. Theoretically speaking, that is. It wouldn't be polite."

"Agreed. And we both know I'm nothing if not polite." Considering their rocky beginnings, with his being pushy, demanding and rude and her giving him a taste of his own medicine right back, his absurd comment hit the mark and she laughed. He joined her. Good. She had a sense of humor. He'd try to keep her smiling, because she really was gorgeous to watch that way. "Truth is, since adopting Dani I don't get out much anymore. So are you really up for this?"

"Absolutely. But who'll watch Dani?"

Thoughtful of her to wonder. "I'll ask Cat again, since I haven't introduced him to Thai food yet." *And I'd like time alone with you.*

"Okay. Theoretically, that sounds good."

"Yeah, some Dutch beer, coconut curry—heaven."

"I know it's a gazillion calories, but I prefer Thai iced tea."

"Chicks." He tossed his paper napkin across the remaining half of his salad. "Only a lady would pass up good Dutch beer for sweet tea." He wasn't sure why he liked to tease her so much, but the instant she grinned he remembered. They were having something he'd almost forgotten. Fun.

"My prerogative." She feigned being insulted. "And guys. Always competitive. Please, don't tell me you'll force me into a hot curry tasting contest. I'm not one of your brothers."

He leaned forward and gazed into her truly enticing eyes. "How do you know us so well? You have a bunch of brothers, too?"

She shook her head. "Nope. I'm an only child."

"Really? I don't know many of those. What's it like to have a house all to yourself. To know what the sound of a pin dropping is? To never have to cross your legs and dance around in the hallway, waiting for the bathroom?"

After a brief and polite smile on the last comment she went serious, met his gaze and held it. "Lonely?"

That answer made him sad. He knew that kind of loneliness, plus fear, having been left alone at night for a couple of years before he'd been taken away from his mother—he hated the memory and tried to suppress it as much as possible—plus, he wanted to put a positive spin on the conversation to keep things upbeat. "And quiet. I bet it was really quiet at your house, you lucky dog." Though the quiet used to scare him to death as that left-behind kid.

She'd finished her lunch and moved her salad bowl away to prove it. "So you grew up in a noisy house, big deal. Isn't that why they invented earbuds and playlists?"

Being around her kept him from going to that old and awful place in his mind.

"Headphones back then at my house with portable CD players. And anytime I used them one of my brothers would sneak up and pull them off my head. Made me all flinchy, waiting. Couldn't even enjoy the music."

He'd made her laugh lightly again and he really appreciated her putting up with his silliness, because he needed to get far away from bad memories. The fact that he'd fudged about his "family" really being a foster family didn't seem relevant now. "You know, if I didn't have to get back to work, I'd invite you to have lunch there right now."

"But I've already had lunch. Just finished."

She tipped her head, a suspicious gaze, clueing him in that he needed to do something. After all this big buildup about the great Thai food, the almost-but-not-quite invitation, he'd better make his move beyond the theoretical. And as his foster father used to say, there was no time like the present.

"Will you have dinner with me tomorrow night, then? I'm thinking Thai food. Hollywood. Beer or iced tea, but definitely fried bananas for dessert." He'd just asked out the first woman after his breakup with Katie and becoming a father, and it felt damn good. He was ready for this. Except maybe he should hold off on the triumph part until he got her answer.

A why-not expression brightened her rich mocha eyes, but only after a long moment's hesitation. This one wasn't looking for a date or a boyfriend—a good thing in general, but right this moment a little unnerving. "Sure," she said finally. "I'd like that."

Both surprised and happy, he grinned and rapped his knuckles twice on the cafeteria tabletop. "Great. It's a date, then."

"I'm sorry, Mom," Andrea said over the phone after lunch. "I've just made plans for tomorrow night." Why she'd agreed to have dinner with Sam Marcus was beyond her, but he'd lured her with a great-sounding meal, and to be honest the thought of spending a few hours with him hadn't seemed like such a bad idea at the time. Not even fifteen minutes later she doubted her decision.

Chalk another one up to dear old Dad, the first and worst man in her life.

"With a man?" Mom didn't even try to hide her surprise.

Andrea snickered. Yes, it was a rare occurrence for her to accept dates, so she couldn't blame her mother's honest outburst. Jerome Rimmer had done a number on both of them. "Yes, Mother, a man." A doctor, no less. Was she crazy?

"Well, that's wonderful."

"I don't know about wonderful, but there is Thai food involved, so it won't be all bad." No, she wasn't looking for a relationship, that was for sure, especially not with a doctor. Her overbearing, demanding, perfectionist father had pretty much messed her up forever in the male/female department. But a simple evening out, gazing at a way more than decent-looking guy, who also happened to smell really good—she couldn't help noticing during lunch—wouldn't be a total loss of an evening, would it?

"Oh, now, Andrea, maybe he'll be nice."

And maybe Dad was actually the greatest guy on earth,

but somehow Andrea had never noticed it before? "He seems nice. But let's not read more into this than necessary. I'm making an eye for his adopted son, so I think he may just want to pay me back somehow."

"Oh, I see." Mom went quiet.

Her mother rarely invited Andrea to dinner, but now that she was on the new medicine regimen for her debilitating depression, she seemed to have more energy and to be more interested in interacting with people. Andrea hated to put her off. "Can we get together Friday night?"

"Oh, Friday is a bad night for your father. He's got a weekend conference to attend in Sacramento and he's leaving that afternoon."

"We could make it a girls' night out, just the two of us." Andrea had learned as a child how fragile her mother was emotionally, especially after marrying a guy like Andrea's dad, and her insecurity about being loved was still a weakness. The last thing Andrea wanted to do was blow her off without making replacement plans. Besides, she'd much rather have dinner with just her mother than both of her parents.

"That might be fun, but let me fix dinner," her mother said. "We can stay in and eat here."

Aware that her mother was still dealing with her reclusiveness and anxiety issues, Andrea wouldn't push it. "That's fine. I just want to spend time with you. Plus you know I love your cooking." Growing up, watching her mother always trying to impress her father with her cooking skills but always coming up short for her perfectionistic father, had taught Andrea not to even try to learn to cook.

"I'll keep it simple, but it will be great to see you. Seems like forever." Her mother's "simple" was fifty times better than anything Andrea could come up with.

"Barbara! Where's my gray tie? Did you iron those

shirts for me?" Andrea's father's voice boomed in the background, demanding as always.

"Oh! Um, let me do that right now," Barbara said, her voice shifting toward trying-to-please mode from the relaxed state a second before. "I've got to go, honey. See you Friday. I'll tell Dad you said hi."

"I'll bring dessert!" She'd buy it from the local bakery.

And that was that. Dad bellowed, Mom jumped. Too bad antidepressants couldn't change that well-worn routine, too. And for the record, she hadn't said hi to her dad.

Sam picked up Andrea after work on Thursday, having removed his tie from a gray denim shirt and wearing a sporty black lightweight zip-up jacket and dark jeans. She'd dressed nicer than usual for work, had even worn wedge-heeled sandals, knowing tonight was their date, and had rushed to change when the department closed. She'd hoped her straight-legged beige pants and gentle yellow boat-necked sweater would be nice enough for dinner out, and, seeing his casual appearance, she decided she'd made the right decision.

"Hey." His genuine expression gave her the impression he was happy, and maybe a little excited about seeing her.

She was flat-out nervous, since he was the first guy she'd wanted to go out with in months, and worked hard to cover her nervousness and focus on the meal part, not the date. "Hi. I'm starving—how about you?"

"Definitely. Hmm, you smell great."

"Thanks. Sometimes I worry I smell like acrylics and wax after working here all day. I didn't overdo it, did I?" She'd used a sample she'd gotten at a cosmetic counter the last time she'd bought eyeliner. It had an almost stringent citrusy scent in the container, but softened on her skin. Or at least she hoped so.

He stepped closer and sniffed the air, but she got the

distinct impression he'd wanted to test her neck, which kind of excited her. "Smells great to me."

Their eyes connected and something fizzed through her body. "Thanks." She pretended to hunt for her purse while she regained her composure. What was it about Dr. Sam Marcus that shook her up so much, especially since she'd seen him in another light at his house? This guy wasn't all boom and bluster, like her father. He was obviously a caring father who'd taken in a special-needs kid. One of the good guys, and good guys were even scarier than the bastards.

When they arrived at the Thai restaurant, it was only six, but the place was already crowded. Wall-to-wall tables lined up with little care for intimacy, just straight row after row from one end to the other of the modern Asian eatery. Though there were more secluded tables outside, enclosed by an intricate white wrought-iron fence to separate them from the boulevard, Sam thought the street noise would be too distracting and said so. So they took a table inside by a window with tall bamboo on the other side.

"It's not much for ambiance, but I endorse the food one hundred percent."

"I can't wait."

They grinned at each other all through dinner. Sam obviously enjoyed his Dutch beer, and Andrea savored her sweet Thai iced tea. She liked the end-of-day stubble on his cheeks and chin, and how his hair wasn't neatly combed. She thought the creases around his mouth made him look distinguished, but the one-sided dimple kept him cute, all-American-boy cute. She'd never call him classically handsome because he had so much more appeal as a good-looking, everyday kind of guy. The part of his face she hesitated to study was his eyes. Those baby blues seemed to reach right inside her whenever they talked, and she got occasional prickles down the back of her neck. It was a feeling she'd nearly forgotten, that "thing" that only certain men set off. Between eating all the great food, their conversation still managed to be nonstop.

Who'd have thought a stuffy, overbearing doctor could be so easy to talk to?

"No, no. I can't," she said, when he offered her one last bite of the fried bananas. "I'll burst." She was definitely thankful she'd worn her semi-loose envelope-hem sweater.

So he popped the last bite into his mouth and chomped down, shaking his head over how good it tasted. He sat back in his chair. "Do I look like a satisfied man? I'm just asking."

His frequent, silly outbursts always made her grin. "You definitely look like a man who's enjoyed his food so much he has a bright yellow curry stain above his pocket."

He pulled in his chin and glanced down, then frowned. "I swear, I think Dani's eating habits are wearing off on me." He dipped his cloth napkin into the remaining glass of water and attempted to do a quick cleanup, which only drew more attention to the stain, which struck her as downright sweet.

"Dr. Sammy! Dr. Sammy!" A high-pitched child's voice cut into the moment. Sam lifted his brows and followed the sound.

So his patients call him Dr. Sammy, how adorable. Could this man be any more appealing?

"Hi!" He waved at a little redheaded boy who looked no more than eight, as he walked by with his parents on their way to being seated. The mother stopped.

"That new medicine you prescribed has done wonders."

Like a true gentleman, "Dr. Sammy" stood and spoke quietly to the boy's mom, though briefly. Andrea looked on with a strange feeling growing inside. Admiration. This was a good guy who took his job seriously, and who didn't just talk the talk but walked the walk. He cared about people. He was single and he'd adopted a son. With his profession, he could have indulged himself with everything from travel to grown-up toys like cars and boats to women, but he'd chosen to go on medical mission trips, settle down and raise a son...who'd lost his eye and needed special care. She'd never met a man like Dr. Sammy before.

The negative side of her allowed one little thought to slip past. What was the catch? Was he too good to be true? Maybe she'd seen the real Dr. Marcus the first day she'd met him, and for her taste that'd been way too much like dear old Dad. Maybe he was on his best behavior tonight and it was all a facade.

Andrea hated how her father still negatively influenced her life and her thinking toward men.

She took one last drink from her tea and stood when Sam offered her his hand. "We ready?"

"I'm going to have to waddle out of here," she said, "but, yes, thanks."

The odd thing was he didn't let go of her hand as they walked back to the car. The warmth of his solid palm flat against hers turned out to be far more distracting than the loud car noises, brakes and horns along Hollywood Boulevard, or the ugly earlier memories of being raised by a man like Dad. Sam's grip felt warm, and if hands could actually do this, it also felt sexy. She pursed her lips, wondering what to make of everything.

Sam walked Andrea to the apartment door. The sturdy Spanish-styled beige triplex dwelling had two units downstairs and a larger single unit upstairs. Andrea's was on the lower right, with rustic red Saltillo tile on the entry porch and an azalea shrub in a huge terra-cotta container right next to the door. He'd been surprised to learn she often took public transportation to work, and he wondered happily if maybe today she'd chosen to do it because they'd had plans for dinner and she wanted a ride home from him. He wouldn't let that fact go to his head, but it sure made his outlook optimistic about what might come next.

"Would you like to come in?"

Of course! "Sure. Thanks."

She unlocked the solid dark wooden door and flipped on lights. The funky yet hip apartment showed a different side of the Andrea he'd come to know at the hospital. The walls were covered in paintings that he knew for a fact he couldn't afford, and he wondered how she could. Rather than sit down in one of the boxy chairs or on the trendy urban home-styled sofa, he walked around the room and admired each one of the amazing conceptual modern paintings that featured mostly bright colors and abstract designs and patterns. "These are something else."

"Thanks."

Then his eyes caught sight of another one, very different from the others, in a corner by itself. It was a long rectangular canvas featuring a single eye peeking through a keyhole in an old door. From his own reading on the topic, he recognized this style as something called photorealism. "I'd buy something like this. It's really special." It spoke to him, seemed to nail how he'd felt as a foster kid at first, watching life through a keyhole, not really a part of it. Sometimes he still felt that way.

"Thank you."

"Who painted all of these?" He squinted to read the tiny signature but couldn't quite make it out.

"Oh, let's see. Um, me." She pointed to one of the bigger paintings, then another. "Me. Oh, and me and me." She ended by pointing to the door and keyhole, his favorite. "Me."

He did a double take and his brows had to have risen a good inch. "Wow. You're really talented." *She's an artist?* Hadn't he sworn off the artistic types after Katie, the actress, had chosen a recurring bit part on a TV sitcom to being his wife and an adoptive mother? "Now I get why you were reading that book on Jackson Pollock yesterday." Andrea possessed significant talent, he couldn't deny that.

"I don't paint anything like him, but I love his renegade approach to art." She threw her jacket over a chair. "He inspires me to take chances."

"So, let me get this straight. You're an artist who works at the hospital, making prosthetic eyes for people."

"Correct."

"But—" he glanced around at the spectacular paintings "—painting is your first love."

She stopped and sighed. "I have to be honest and say yes."

Uh-oh. Been there with Katie. "So if a millionaire bought all of your paintings, you'd walk out the door of St. Francis of the Valley and never look back?"

She stood perfectly still, clearly weighing the truth of her answer. Her eyes drifted over the walls of her apartment, studying her own work for just a moment. "In a perfect world, yes. But I have a grandmother I respect and a father who would hound me to death if I dared. And, honestly, I love my patients and the fact that I can improve their lives."

He didn't like the sound of the first part of her answer one bit. It meant she worked in the O&A department against her will. In fact, he hated the answer so much that a yellow flag waved in the recesses of his mind. Artists were flighty. People you couldn't depend on. Sign him on to the grandmother and dad's side. The thought didn't seem fair to Andrea, though. It felt kind of selfish, if he was honest, but after his experience with Katie his perspective was blurred. Then there was the second part of her answer—she loved helping people and obviously got a lot out of the job in that respect. Life was never black-and-white, and in her case he preferred the gray areas.

There was something about Andrea that called out to him. He genuinely liked her, she was attractive, talented, fun to be around, and she gave a damn about people. She also happened to turn him on. Very much. His instinct said to go for it, kiss her. Damn. Why couldn't he think straight? He'd blame it on the carb high from the Thai food, but the concern about her being an artist was still enough to trip him up.

"Would you like some coffee or wine?"

"The wine sounds great, but can I take a rain check? I need to pick up Dani." His son was a logical excuse, and an honest one. He really did need to go get him.

Sam glanced around the living room. He liked the feel of her home, especially liked her, and would've liked to stick around, yellow flag or not, because she was so damn hot. But he was a father and knew for a fact that Dani slept best in his own bed. Which was a great argument for finding a babysitter besides his foster sister—who couldn't do nights—one who would come to his house. Being a parent, especially a single father, had been a steep learning curve, and this moment had just taught him something else, besides caution about the new lady in his world—the value of a teenage, pay-by-the-hour babysitter. Did they still exist? He'd make a mental note to follow up on the idea ASAP so he wouldn't have to miss out on another invitation like this from Andrea, if she ever gave him one.

He noticed Andrea's disappointment over his rain check on the wine. It was in her nearly Keane-like eyes, which surprised and pleased him at the same time. Was she as interested in him as he was in her?

But she recovered quickly. "Sure. After that huge dinner I should put some time in on the treadmill anyway. A glass of wine would definitely interfere with that."

He'd enjoyed every second of watching her tonight over dinner. She'd eaten like a champ, and she'd parted her hair on the side and swept her bangs, the only long part of her hair, to one side, accenting her round face, big eyes and sharp chin. The short-haired style was definitely growing on him. She'd held up her end of the conversation throughout the evening, too, and he'd never felt the need to fill in lag time. She hadn't said a thing about her talent, either. Humble. Another good trait.

It made sense that a trained artist would be right for the job of re-creating eyes, and he assumed every eye was unique in some way, and an artist would be best to detect the difference. Now he was glad grandmother Judith had assigned her to his son's case. Glancing around her walls at the bright colors and splotches of paint that, though seeming random, still managed to grab an immediate reaction from him, he realized that Andrea was special, someone he wanted to know more. Even though he'd been kicked hard in the relationship solar plexus by Katie. Andrea was different. He had to keep that in mind.

Hell, Cat would be the first to chew him out for comparing the two women. And he didn't know Andrea well enough to pigeonhole her anyway, but she'd admitted art was her first love. She'd be willing to walk away from ocularistry if the artistic opportunity arose. Theoretically. But why should that matter? He wanted to get to know her better, and that part, the glutton-for-punishment part, the part that still insisted women didn't stick around for him, made him nervous. All because she was so damn appealing.

He was a father now, with a son who needed much of his attention and a job that needed the rest. Was there even room for a woman?

The silent pause had grown long and awkward. He'd been overthinking things, like always. That was another thing that being a foster kid had taught him—consider all possibilities, because life could change at a moment's notice. "I guess I better be going."

"Okay," she muttered, resigned. Disappointed? He hoped so because he sure was.

"Nice apartment, by the way," he said, thinking how lame he sounded, and turned to leave.

Andrea strode toward him with those crazy-sexy platform sandals tapping on the Spanish tile and something on her mind, and he stopped dead in his tracks. If he wasn't mistaken, she was giving a clear sign, so when she got close enough he held her upper arms and moved in for a kiss that evidently she had already been planning on. Great, the feeling *was* mutual. But was he sure it was a good idea?

Right now, who cared?

Her hands wrapped around his neck and that sexy fragrance he'd picked up on back at the hospital lingered in the air. He liked it. A lot. Her mouth felt fresh, tasted sweet, like her tea, and full of life. Every worry about her being an artist flew from his head. She kissed like a curious explorer, and he dived in with enthusiasm and soon did some serious investigating of his own. He liked the warmth of the inside rim of her lips, the feel of them on his, the fact that she opened her mouth and invited him in, then put him under her spell. She was a creative kisser, as she was a creative painter, and he soon got swept away.

With her body pressed against his, her heat and softness melding to his chest, a forgotten hunger came out of hiding. He wanted more of her. Confusion about pursuing his lust and whether it would be wise or not, and the more practical need to pick up his son at a reasonable hour, soon crept back into his thoughts and ruined the moment. He couldn't get carried away now. Was she trying to seduce him? Or had he made way too much out of her inviting kisses? She was a naturally passionate person, probably couldn't control it, so it made sense that she'd kiss like this. He was the one who'd blown everything way out of proportion because he was so out of practice, and still smarting, thanks to Katie. He cupped Andrea's soft cheeks and regretfully ended the kiss.

Neither said a word. He stared at her warm brown eyes and she stared back. The unspoken, mutual message being *Wow*. Yeah, there was definitely something there. Something between them. Sparks and fireworks and all. He couldn't very well jump into the sack with her, as he might have done back in medical school, not now that he was thirty-five, and a father, but he definitely knew, good idea or bad, he wanted to, and that was definitely a step forward.

"Will you have dinner with me tomorrow night?" he asked, his voice throaty with desire.

Her eyes went bigger, as if they could, and she smiled. Something told him to sell the deal, just in case there was any hesitation on her part about seeing a new guy two nights in a row. Three if they counted the night she'd measured Dani for his prosthetic eye. Oh, and lunch yesterday… But who was counting?

"I'm a great cook, and I plan to dazzle you with my culinary skills. And after Dani goes to bed, we can do more of this." He kissed her lightly but, practicing restraint, only once.

Her eyes went dreamy. Good, she liked his pitch.

"I'd love to but I've made plans with my mother for tomorrow night. I'm sorry."

What? At least she hadn't blown him off outright, but plans with her mother?

"Would Saturday work?" she said, before he had the chance to think any further.

"It does. As a matter of fact, it does." The blush on her

cheeks may have been fading, but he was glad he'd put it there in the first place, and he was especially happy about her taking him up on his invitation, even if it was a day later.

Yeah, he was in trouble.

"Then I'll see you at seven on Saturday. How's that?"

"I'll be there."

He wasn't sure what he was getting himself into, seeing a woman—a yellow-flag-raising woman—several nights in a row, and maybe taking Friday night off would be a good thing, to cool down, but right at this exact moment he liked the possibilities.

"That was the greatest meal I've ever had," Andrea said on Saturday night, wiping her mouth with a paper napkin and pushing back from the table. "Even counting the Thai food Thursday night."

"You're awfully easy to please," Sam said, smiling. They were sitting at the small round table in the kitchen alcove, and he loved it that she liked his cooking. "Since it's the weekend I probably should have made something fancier."

"Are you kidding? I loved the shepherd's pie. The chicken was a nice switch, the spring vegetables were fresh, and I could tell your crust was homemade."

"You're okay with a guy who makes his own crust?" It was one of the first ways he'd bonded with his foster mom, by helping out in the kitchen. He'd wanted to be that good, likable boy whom they wouldn't send back, and helping in the kitchen had paid off. Not that they'd ever threatened or anything, but he'd been sent to a couple other foster homes before he'd wound up at the Murphys'.

Andrea gave a quick throaty laugh, one he'd already come to like. "I don't cook, so any homemade meal is a treat."

She didn't cook? Being artistic, he'd half expected her to be a gourmet chef, even worried she'd find his basic home cooking boring. Turned out that line of thinking had been a waste of time, since he was the one with the kitchen skills. "Then I'm especially glad you enjoyed it." He pushed another tiny yellow waving flag to the back of his brain. One: artist. Two: doesn't cook. And changed the subject.

"See, Dani? She cleaned her plate."

The little boy had eaten less than half of his dinner when he'd pushed away his bowl. Sam, being a pediatrician and often reassuring stressed-out mothers that their picky eaters were getting all the nutrition they needed, had been suffering from the same worries where Dani was concerned. The boy's all-time favorite meal was white rice. Period. Where was the nutrition in that?

"You sure you don't want another bite of baby carrot and new potato?" Sam remained hopeful Dani might want to show off for his new friend Andrea, but Dani shook his head vigorously, lips sealed tight.

Andrea scooted her chair closer to Dani in his booster seat. She picked up his fork and put a small mouthful of food on it, then made a buzzing sound and moved the fork around like an airplane. She lifted it upward, and Dani followed it with his one good eye, then to the right and the left. Dani might not be sure what was going on but she definitely kept his attention.

"Open wide for the landing," she said, buzzing and moving the fork in concentric circles toward his face.

Amazingly, Dani opened his mouth and let her place the food inside.

"You're good at that," she said, grinning. "Can you do it yourself?" Without waiting for his answer, she speared another small bite of dinner with his fork, but this time handed it over to Dani. "Bzzzzz," she began, and Dani moved his fork up then down, then around and round and right into his mouth. He laughed, mouth full of food and all, and Andrea clapped.

"You really are good at that. Want to do it again?" she said, sitting pertly on the edge of the chair in her layered tank tops of orange and blue, looking as colorful as one of her paintings.

Dani agreed to a third bite, but after that he was through, and she didn't push him. Good for her. She glanced at Sam and he nodded at her secret message. Yup, that was three more bites eaten that neither of them— them being him or Dani—had expected. Evidently, with the satisfied smile perched on that lovely mouth of hers, she'd never had a doubt it wouldn't work.

Sam had no sooner subtracted points from Andrea's scoreboard for not being a cook than he added some back for helping Dani eat, and several more for being so damn sweet about it. Not to mention the bonus points for being so easy on the eyes and the fact she was a damn good kisser. Sam stood to clear the table, and hopefully clear his head. Andrea had him all mixed up.

"Let me do that," she said, hopping up and taking the dishes from his hands. "It's the least I can do to thank you."

He stopped himself from making a wisecrack about not having a stool for her to stand on at the sink, choosing instead to enjoy having a woman like Andrea in his home, bringing such warmth and fun along with her. "Okay, if you insist."

She tossed him a sassy glance. "I do." Then she moseyed off to the kitchen sink, swaying her jeans-clad hips in an exaggerated manner. He and Dani weren't the only ones having a good time. The thought squeezed his heart the slightest bit. Was it a good idea to let Dani fall for her right along with him?

"Well, in that case, come on, Dani, are you ready for your bath?" He helped his son down from the booster seat and Dani ran straight for the hall.

"Yay, bath!"

"Be careful, remember the bookcase," Sam couldn't stop himself from warning Dani about the furniture, since they were still working on his loss of vision on the left.

Dani pretended to run into the wall, then made a big deal about faking falling down.

"You character," Sam said, grinning.

The boy got up again, squealed with delight and, having clearly gotten his dad's approval, ran into the opposite wall on purpose.

"You're a silly, silly guy, you know that?" Sam said, laughing and playing along with Dani all the way toward the bathroom. Realizing that his son most likely did it to impress Andrea, Sam shook his head. *Guys, even little guys, can't resist showing off for pretty ladies.* That moment of understanding, that Dani was a little guy who would one day become a man and who deserved all the fun stuff in life, just like anyone else, circled Sam's chest with warmth.

That clench of the heart from earlier squeezed about ten times harder. No matter how many times Sam had doubted himself about adopting Dani, the boy always proved what a perfect decision it had been. Adoption was just like a marriage vow, in sickness and in health. They were on this road together, and Sam never intended to let him down. The same way Mom Murphy had thought about him and the other foster kids she'd brought into her home. Damn, he missed her.

As he walked down the hall, just before he reached the bathroom he glanced back toward the kitchen. A whistling and singing-under-her-breath picture of beauty, Andrea stood at the sink as she organized the dishes and ran steamy, soapy water. Then he applauded himself for making another spot-on decision—asking her over for dinner tonight.

And God help him if he was setting himself up for another fall.

CHAPTER FOUR

ANDREA WORKED DILIGENTLY, polishing the clear acrylic replica of Dani's eye shape, taken from the mold in her office workshop. The sooner he was fitted, the sooner she'd know if the prosthetic was comfortable and therefore functional for a healthy and active growing child. The month-long adjustment period was probably the most important step in the process.

Then she'd begin delicately painting the subtle characteristics of his individual iris. The series of photographs she'd taken the other night were posted on her computer screen for her to zoom in on and examine. Everything from color patterns, striations and flecks would be replicated in Dani's final prosthesis. Even now red embroidery string had been draped in the configuration of minute red vessels on the white blob that would soon become Dani's sclera.

Sure, there was a new push for digitized replications for prosthetic eyes, but her grandmother was strictly old-school, and that'd made Andrea, even at the age of twenty-eight, an old-school diehard, too. Though she admitted to being interested in the new process popping up around the country. If it meant getting more high-quality eyes to more people in an efficient manner, it might be worth looking into.

When she hooked up the acrylic to a muslin-mopped buffing machine, her mind wandered.

A shiver snaked down her spine as she remembered the time-stopping kiss she'd shared with Sam on Saturday night. They'd been spending a lot of time kissing over the past few days. He was a good kisser. While they'd lingered in their lip-lock she'd explored the strength of his shoulders and chest, resisting the urge to continue on down his frame to his butt. That was definitely territory she hoped to check out in the near future. If she played her cards right...

A countertop pressure cooker dinged. An eye her grandmother had been working on had cured to rubbery toughness, so she took it out. With Andrea's thoughts securely back on the business of prosthetics and Dani, warmth opened and spread like a big floppy flower in her chest as she thought about her growing crush on the boy. He was so trusting and sweet and, well, she'd gone and let him steal her heart. A smile, urged on by tender thoughts, spread across her face until she thought about Sam and jitters replaced that warm fuzzy feeling. Would it be wise to fall for a highly driven doctor, like her father? She knew firsthand the consequences of stepping into that situation. What about Dani? Would he grow up feeling the way she had all her life, second best to his father's profession?

She thought about how caring Sam was with Dani, how attentive and alert to his needs he'd been that night. And after putting Dani to bed, how attentive he'd been to her. Another shiver shot down her spine. No. He was nothing like her father. That guy she'd met the first day here in the office had been an aberration. His son had just had surgery! He'd been stressed to his limit, and she hadn't helped the situation one iota. Of course they'd gotten off on the wrong foot.

Sam was *nothing* like Jerome Rimmer.

Her office desk phone rang.

"Hey," Sam said on the other end.

"Hi!" *I was just thinking about you.*

"I had a minute and wanted to call."

Because he was thinking about her, too? "I'm glad you did. I'm working on Dani's acrylic and need to fit him again."

"I'll ask Cat to bring him in, if that's okay."

"Of course. You've got a busy schedule."

"And it just got busier. Have you read the newspaper today?"

"Haven't had a chance yet." It wasn't a part of her routine because national news always depressed her.

"I'm part of a medical mission group, that's how I met Dani, and we try to set up clinics at least once a year wherever we're needed. I just got an email that our scheduled trip got postponed because of the drug cartel activity in Mexico, and they want to discuss it at a last-minute meeting tonight. I've been so busy with Dani I'd forgotten all about it. Anyway, I'm going to have to go to a meeting tonight." He went quiet.

She caught on to where he was going with the conversation. "And you need me to watch Dani?"

"As a matter of fact…"

After all the swooning thoughts she'd had about the boy, not to mention Sam, she didn't need to think. "I'd be happy to. That means I get to see Dani." *And maybe kiss you again.*

"Thank you so much." She heard pure relief in his voice.

On the verge of saying "Anytime," she stopped herself. She'd already just jumped right in and offered to babysit without giving it a second thought. She didn't want to be taken for granted. "You're welcome."

"Is six-thirty okay? I'll try to have him bathed and ready for bed by then."

Again, she stopped herself from saying "No problem, I can do it" and instead went the efficient route. "That works for me."

"Can you stick around afterward?" His tone had gone quiet. Sexy. "Let's take that rain check on wine and.." Hadn't they already done that on Saturday night? But who was counting? She'd gladly keep rain checking over and over.

"Ah, sweetening the pot, I see. Now I'm all in." How was a living, breathing woman supposed to resist that kind of invitation and not play along?

His low, sexy-as-hell rumble of a laugh nearly had her hanging up the phone and marching upstairs to Pediatrics so she could plant one major, sloppy kiss on him right then and there to seal their deal.

"I'll see you later, then," he said. "I've got to run now."

"Okay, see you later." After hanging up, she quickly returned to her senses.

Sure, she liked Dani and Sam but things needed to proceed naturally and at their own pace. Plus she didn't want to come off like a welcome mat for Sam to take advantage of. She'd known the guy for a week and was already volunteering to be his babysitter. Sheesh. If she was going to get into a relationship with Sam, it should be for all the right reasons, not because of convenience.

She needed to stay focused and realistic.

Truth was, any night spent with Sam or babysitting Dani was a night away from painting. Since they'd bumped her up to five days a week instead of four in the O&A department, that left the weekends plus weeknights for painting, and she had minimal time for art as it was. Plus she worried about Sam always being taken away from his son. A medical mission meant travel. Who'd take care of Dani? Then it hit her.

Was Sam setting her up for that, too? If not her, how often did Sam expect to ship Dani off to his aunt Cat's? Little Dani had had no say in the adoption, but she was quite sure that wasn't what he'd bargained for. Kids needed their parents around as much as possible. That's how they felt loved. Again, she knew that from personal experience.

Hating how her relationship with her father shadowed her thoughts about Sam, but admitting she had some real concerns about him not being around enough for the boy, she refocused and went back to work on the prosthesis. But this time the job wasn't accompanied by dreamy thoughts or a wistful smile.

The next week…

Dani arrived at Andrea's office for the fine-tuning of the clear acrylic the boy had been wearing in preparation for his permanent prosthetic eye. They'd arranged for an end-of-shift appointment, so once Cat delivered the boy, Andrea could take Dani to Sam after his pediatric clinic ended. They'd also agreed to all have dinner out afterward, nothing fancy or exotic this time, just good old American food for Dani's sake.

Andrea replaced Dani's eye patch and patted his arm. "You're getting used to it?"

The boy shrugged his narrow shoulders.

"Does it bother you?"

"Don't know." He looked at his lap. She realized he didn't understand her questions.

"Does it hurt? Do you want to rub it?" She demonstrated rubbing her eye and made a face as if her eye hurt.

He stared at her with his one beautiful brown eye and slowly shook his head.

"That's good, then I did a good job." She smiled and he smiled back. "Want to go see your dad?"

His face brightened as he nodded exuberantly. After saying goodbye to her grandmother, off they went toward the elevator, Andrea feeling protective of Dani when people noticed his eye patch and reacted with sad pouts or sorry faces. She'd come to know the boy quickly in the past couple of weeks, and already she was attached to him, always eager to see him whenever she saw Sam. She also was beginning to understand Sam's deep concerns, not wanting Dani to see himself as inferior or pitied by others.

After they got out of the elevator on the pediatric clinic floor, they used the back entrance to reach Sam's office. Surprisingly, Sam was sitting at his desk.

He looked up and grinned. "My two favorite people!" he said diplomatically. Andrea knew, hands down, if it came to making a choice Dani would win, but it felt good to be included in Sam's world. With each kiss they seemed to be getting closer to crossing the line to making love. She wondered how that would change the dynamic, between not only her and Sam but her and Dani.

Dani rushed to his dad for a hug and the sight released bubble-like warmth in her chest, all floaty and happy feeling. Sam stood. "How'd the fitting go?"

"I only needed to make tiny adjustments and polish the acrylic. Things are going great. I should be finished with his prosthetic by next week, and after another week we'll replace this one for the real thing." She grinned at Dani. "Then you won't have to wear the patch anymore. Yay."

Dani clapped. After smiling at her tiny patient, her gaze drifted toward Sam. He must have really liked what she'd said because he bore a look that mixed practical appreciation with nothing less than smoldering desire. What a combo! It set off a sparkling cascade across her shoulders and breasts, and she knew for a fact her peaked breasts pointed against the thin material of her blouse. It didn't go unnoticed. He stepped toward her, put his hand behind her neck and gently brought her within kissing range. His eyes flickered with pure desire just before their lips met.

It may have been a clinical office kiss but, wow, it thrummed right through her center straight down to her nearly curling toes. There they lingered on the outskirts of heaven until Dani tugged on both of their slacks and put a swift end to the moment, but not before Andrea saw a promise for much, much more…later. And she was definitely ready for that next step. Had been almost since the first night they'd kissed. Sam was a man she wanted to know completely, big scary doctor or not.

"I just finished my last appointment…" There was that post-kiss huskiness in his voice she'd come to love.

"Dr. Sammy!" A nurse appeared at his door. "There's a little girl having an acute asthma attack in the waiting room."

He instantly snapped out of their promising romantic moment. "Bring her to my exam room."

Andrea stepped aside and gathered Dani to her legs as "Dr. Sammy" strode out the door.

Down the hall, another nurse rushed in, with a panic-stricken mother following behind holding a limp child with her head on her mother's shoulder. "The urgent care triage nurse said she didn't hear any wheezing, so I left, but this happened before we got to the car."

Sam knew that wasn't always a good sign. The urgent care nurse may have heard a "quiet chest" but for all the wrong reasons. If the child had been suffering from a prolonged asthma attack, it may have turned into status asthmaticus, where the lungs had shut down, which could lead to imminent respiratory failure and, if not treated, cardiac arrest.

He strode to the exam room and saw a cyanotic toddler being propped up in a sitting position by her mother. The little girl used the accessory muscles of her upper chest, trying to breathe. When he had the mother remove the child's shirt, retraction was obvious between her ribs. The child was in acute respiratory distress. He instructed his nurse to measure the pulse oximetry, then put oxygen on the patient immediately.

"Mom, has she had a virus recently?" He pulled out his stethoscope, preparing to listen to the child's lungs. "Had to use inhalers more often? Been treated with steroids lately?"

"Yes," the stressed mother said, sounding as breathy as her child. "Last week. I knew I had to bring her to you, Dr. Marcus, but your appointments were full."

He shook his head, wishing for more time in the day and more appointment slots for kids like this, but also in disappointment over the UC triage missing the bigger picture than lungs without noticeable wheezing. They were supposed to be the safety net for situations like these, but today they'd let a patient and her mother down.

The pulse oximeter indicated a hypoxic patient with a loud alarm. Sam sighed at the reading. "Get a mask on her at eight liters. Start a line," he said to his nurse Leslie. "I'm going to give her a pop of adrenaline. Mom, how much does she weigh?"

The mother told him and he made quick mental calculations and drew up the drug, hoping to buy time before they set up a nebulizer treatment. He delivered the intramuscular injection, then stuck his head out of the examination room door. "Sharon? We need more hands in here." From the corner of his eye, he saw movement and turned toward Andrea and Dani. Concern covered her face.

"I'm going to take Dani home with me," she said, her brow furrowed.

He gave a grateful nod, trying to offer reassurance, but honestly he hadn't a clue how things would turn out for the little girl. "I'll come later as soon as I can. Thanks."

They left the department just before the tiny asthmatic took another step for the worse.

"Let's nebulize some adrenaline, try to open her up, then start the bronchodilator—oh, and add some ipratropium bromide, too." Why did he have the feeling he was running a precode? He studied the limp child. "Got that line in yet, Leslie?" His major hope was that her veins hadn't collapsed.

The nurse had just finished opening the tubing and the fluid flowed into the vein in the child's antecubital fossa. "Let's titrate terbutaline." He did quick mental math for kilograms of weight, then gave the amount for the piggyback to the IV. "Call the pharmacy, tell them we need methylprednisolone IV for a thirty-five-pound child, stat.

"Sharon, have someone call Respiratory, get someone up here pronto for blood gases." So far none of their efforts had increased the child's O2 sat, and if things continued on this trajectory they might soon be dealing with a code blue. "We'll keep the respiratory therapist around in case we need to intubate."

And so it went…

Andrea drove Dani slowly to her house, worried about not having a car seat for him and making him sit in the backseat of her car with the seat belt buckled tight. What would Sam have done if she hadn't been there? That wasn't all she worried about. Every time she'd seen him over the past three weeks, with each kiss she'd felt herself slip closer and closer to falling for him. Just now, seeing Sam spring into action like a hero for a child in need helped her understand how dedicated he was to his profession.

It also helped her put her own situation into perspective.

Seeing his unwavering commitment forced her to take a good long look at herself, and how unsure she still was about her own professional path. She seemed to be standing with one foot in ancillary medicine and the other in the creative arts. And the truth was she loved both! Straddling the line hadn't paid off with her painting, she hadn't completed a picture in months, and it kept her anxious and unsatisfied when she worked her forty hours a week in the O&A department. She should never have agreed to add that extra day.

Add in starting to fall for a guy with a demanding job and an adorable kid who needed attention, and she nearly panicked, feeling completely out of control of her own situation. How had she let this happen? Sam had a way of taking over, just like her father, even when it wasn't obvious. Was that how it had all started with her mother? Little by little, because her mother hadn't figured out where she wanted to be in life, Jerome had taken over until there seemed nothing left of her mother. Until she'd practically disappeared!

Could the same happen to *her*?

"I'm hungry," Dani said from the backseat.

Thank goodness he'd broken her negative train of thought. "Want a hamburger?"

He clapped. "Yes!"

At least some decisions were still easy to make.

Fortunately, Cat had delivered Dani's day bag with him when she'd brought him by that afternoon. Andrea found pajamas and a pair of clean underpants plus some kids' books inside and so much more. Even Ribbit, the stuffed frog she'd given him. She'd been able to bathe him and read a book that apparently was his favorite, *Goodnight California*.

The author used the *Goodnight Moon* setup to say

good-night in travelogue style to all the beautiful places in the state. Dani sat rapt, holding Ribbit, snuggled under her arm on the sofa, listening to every word as if he'd never heard them before, and pointing to his favorite pictures. The redwoods, Yosemite, the beach. Ah, the beach probably reminded him of home in the Philippines. She wondered if Sam had taken Dani to the beach yet.

Dani's day bag even had a toothbrush, so after one last glass of milk, where Andrea opened up Dani's world to the graham cracker experience of dipping them into the milk, she brushed his teeth and put him to bed, along with Ribbit, in her studio, which had a daybed and trundle bed combo left over from her childhood. Nowadays she used it to flounce onto when she needed to think about what she'd just painted and where to go next, or, as was often the case, to nap on when she'd painted so long she couldn't even bring herself to walk down the hall to her own room. When she'd been a girl, before her mother had gotten really depressed and hadn't allowed her to have friends over, her sleepover guests had got the trundle bed section, and she felt Dani, who had special toddler bed rails at home, would be safe there.

She kissed him good-night and started to tiptoe out of the room.

"Do I live here now?" he asked, just before she shut the door, having left a night-light on in the far corner.

Was that how orphans thought? "No, honey. You're just visiting, like when you go to Aunt Cat's house. Your daddy will come and get you later. But he needed to save a little girl at the hospital first."

"Okay."

It struck like a baseball bat how similar her explanation was to what her mother's used to be on countless nights when her father hadn't made it home in time for dinner or to kiss her good-night. The tender feelings she carried for Dani puffed up and made her eyes prickle.

It was scary to care so much for a little person.

Within a couple of hours of putting Dani to bed, a quiet knock on her door drew her from the art magazine she'd been reading in her living room. She opened the small peephole on the door. It was Sam, looking exactly the way a guy should after having a long, stressful day where lives had been at stake and family responsibilities had had to be put on the back burner. There was a combination of fatigue, guilt and gratefulness she read in his powerful blue gaze.

She invited him in with a quick kiss, pointed to the nearest chair with an ottoman for his feet and offered him a drink of his choice.

"Seems like the perfect time for that rain check on the wine," he said. His shirt collar was unbuttoned and the sight of his throat looked sexy as hell. But, then, she found every little thing about Sam Marcus sexy, she may as well admit it. And she loved the way they'd made an ongoing gag about every glass of wine they shared being a rain check.

"Red or white?"

He closed his eyes on a slow inhalation, as if making one more decision was beyond his grasp, so she solved his problem.

"I've got a fabulous triple red wine open. How does that sound?"

Again, that grateful blue gaze, standing out all the more thanks to the after-five stubble on his cheeks and chin, nearly bowled her over. She turned to fetch the wine when a thought occurred to her. "Have you eaten?"

"No." He didn't need to think long about that.

"I told you I don't cook but I *can* make a pretty good omelet. Would that work?"

"Sounds perfect."

She understood he could probably eat cardboard if he had to by now, as it was almost ten.

"Dani in bed?"

"Yes," she said, as she got down two wineglasses and reached for the bottle on the counter. "Fell right to sleep in my old trundle bed. What a sweetheart he is."

"Okay if I take a peek?"

It was his kid, why did he need to ask? "You're not seriously asking me permission, are you?"

She imagined that Sam Marcus smile she'd come to know and adore spreading across his boyish but all-male face as she poured the wine and he padded down the hall. "Which door?" he asked with a loud whisper.

"First one on the left." She put his glass on the kitchen table and got busy gathering the things she'd need to make her one good dish. Sad but true, her cooking skills didn't go beyond sandwiches and eggs. But she was determined to make the best damn omelet of her life for Sam. She took a quick sip of liquid confidence from the wineglass and went to work.

After a couple of minutes Sam stepped into the kitchen, standing right behind her as she whipped the eggs. He put his hands on her hips, bent and kissed the back of her neck. She nearly dropped the whisk, it felt so heavenly. One touch from Sam. One kiss in the perfect spot, and she was covered in tingles. She stopped what she was doing, leaned back, giving him full access to the side of her neck, and enjoyed every second of this gift as he gently nuzzled and kissed her.

"Thank you," he whispered over the shell of her ear.

More sensations fanned across her scalp, down her neck and over her chest. "Anytime." Whoops, had she just given him permission to leave Dani with her anytime? "I should get this omelet going before you starve to death. Oh, and your wine's on the table."

He let go of her hips and stepped away, and she had dueling thoughts. She was either nuts to let him stop or smart not to let him take advantage of her right there in the kitchen. She took another sip of wine. Yeah, she was probably nuts.

"Good wine," he said.

"I thought you'd like it. How's the little girl?" Listen to them, a regular couple discussing the day and the kids. The thought almost made her smile, but the subject of the little girl fighting for her life kept Andrea serious.

A kitchen chair skidded along the tile as he pulled it out and sat, then took another drink and propped his feet on an adjacent chair. "She's alive, but not in great shape."

Something in Andrea's chest withered with the news as she heated the skillet and oil and when it reached the perfect temperature she poured in the eggs, listening to every word Sam said, giving him time to share as much or as little as he cared to.

"She coded shortly after you left. We intubated her, got her to the ICU in time for a second code." He sighed, and she glanced over her shoulder and saw him rub his temples with his thumb and middle finger. "She's on a ventilator right now, and hopefully the drugs will kick in tonight so we can get her off it as soon as possible."

"Oh, the poor baby." Andrea's insides twisted over the thought of a child fighting for her life. "If her mother hadn't brought her to you, she might be dead."

He nodded deeply and took another drink of wine.

"You look beat. Why don't you go make yourself comfortable on the couch, put your feet up, and I'll bring your dinner as soon as it's done."

He didn't argue, just took his wineglass and left the room. "Good idea."

She flipped the omelet, added grated cheese to the lightly browned side, waited a minute or two for the toast to pop and the eggs to set, then folded the omelet in half and put everything on a plate, then walked to the living room to find Sam asleep on her couch, her everyday hero breathing deep, peaceful breaths that did more for her libido than those butterfly kisses on her neck a few moments ago.

His long, sturdy legs stretched the length of her sofa. He'd kicked off his shoes, his sock-covered feet crossed at the ankles, arms folded over his trim middle, head tilted chin to chest. All he needed was a cowboy hat to complete the picture. He was a fine-looking man, and she could hardly believe he kept coming round. A quick fantasy of crawling like a cat over him and kissing the lips she'd come to long for started a deep yearning to be skin to skin with him. What would it be like?

Truth was she hadn't wanted a man this much since college. The complete opposite of the artsy fellow students she'd dated back then, Sam managed to turn her on wearing, as it happened today, a gray business suit. He hadn't bothered to take off the jacket, so she had to settle for looking at his naked throat and the top of his white undershirt as he slept. *Gimme, gimme.*

She glanced at the plate, steam rising from the best omelet she'd ever concocted especially for Sam, sighed, then took a bite to prove it really was as light and fluffy as it looked. She savored the egg and Cheddar cheese taste and the sight of the man she'd fallen head over heels for in record time passed out from exhaustion on her couch, then made a snap decision.

Tonight was the night.

She tiptoed to the kitchen, found a notepad and scrib-

bled Sam an invitation. Then, making sure to leave one
light on so he'd see it, she propped the note against his
wineglass.

If you want to stay over, I'm keeping the bed warm
for you. My room is at the end of the hall.

CHAPTER FIVE

SAM WOKE UP, a crick in his neck from the awkward position in which he'd fallen asleep on the not-so-soft modern couch. It took a moment to realize where he was. Andrea's cozy triplex apartment. He scrubbed his face to help him wake up. Dani was asleep in her guest bed. Right. No way would he disturb his son at this hour.

He took out his phone and scrolled with blurry vision for any messages from the hospital. He'd signed off with the on-call ICU doc and knew they'd only call with extremely bad news, so he gave a sigh of relief over the lack of "missed call" notices, texts or email.

In the dim light, his gaze drifted to the uneaten omelet on the glass coffee table. It touched him, knowing Andrea was a devout non-cook yet she'd offered to make the one thing she could, especially for him. He felt bad he'd fallen asleep before he could enjoy the fruit of her efforts.

From being so bristly at first, she'd turned out to be the sweetest lady he'd met since Mom Murphy. He thought about reheating the omelet in the microwave and eating it, so her work wouldn't go to waste, plus he really was hungry, but first his vision landed on the wineglass with a propped-up note. He didn't need to pick it up to read: *If you want to stay over, I'm keeping the bed warm for you. My room is at the end of the hall.*

She'd sketched a perfectly sexy eye in mid-wink at the end.

Suddenly wide-awake, Sam gulped down the rest of the red wine, the thought of making love with Andrea foremost on his mind. Hell, yeah, he wanted to. Had since the night he'd first kissed her, right here in her living room, and he remembered every second of that goodbye. Somehow, since then, their make-out sessions had never gotten beyond hot kisses and lots of groping and grabbing.

Why? Not because he hadn't wanted to. No. It was because he'd always sensed Andrea wasn't ready for that. Sure, she'd jump right into making out with him, he never doubted she wanted to. But something about their frantic kisses and fully clothed body sex had always ended with him backing off. Because of one message that always cut through the sexy haze. At some point she'd always tense up and there was no way, no matter how desperate he'd been to have her naked and to be inside her, he would force the next step—getting naked.

Maybe she'd sensed he was the kind of guy who kept his distance. Intimacy, trust, hell, how did a man make heads or tails of that when his own mother had ignored him and let him get taken away? Not to mention Katie leaving when he'd finally felt ready to commit to her.

But there was no doubt about the invitation from Andrea tonight. She was keeping the bed warm for him. It said so right there in her near perfect cursive. An ironic half smile lifted the corner of his mouth. She was an artist, of course she'd have beautiful handwriting, and the artistic winking eye was a great touch. He stuffed the note in his shirt pocket as a reminder. She wanted him.

The thought of her asleep yet waiting for him, her skin warm to his touch, relaxed and completely open, drove a spear of desire straight through him. Fatigued, who? It may have been a long and exhausting day, but he'd had a nap now, and he was fueled by pure desire for Andrea. More than ever he was ready to have his way with his artist.

He stood, took off his jacket, began unbuttoning his shirt and padded in his socked feet straight to her bedroom and the one woman he wanted right now. She'd even left the door open a crack. Once inside, he stripped, leaving a pile of clothes beside her bed before he crawled under the covers.

A blanket of heat and strength spooned behind Andrea as she stirred from her light sleep. Arms enveloped her, pulling her close, igniting excitement and, being honest, fear. She took a trembling breath when Sam kissed the side of her neck, his breathing steady, hot over her ear. She wanted him, God knew she did, so why was she so nervous about making love with him?

Because having sex was a big deal to her, it always had been. She'd tried her share of free and easy dates during college and had always limped away feeling somehow used, or like a user. Need had been a strong stimulant for the "right now" back then, but try as she might she'd always wanted much more. Could she ever actually say she'd loved someone? The truth? Not so far.

She turned toward Sam's chest, letting him capture her mouth with deep kisses as their bodies stretched along each other's. He felt great, every inch of him. Of course she'd gone to bed naked. She couldn't very well leave such a bold-faced invitation and not be ready when or if he took her up on it. She'd even left a condom on the bedside table.

Thankfully, he had followed through, because right now she felt the obvious length of him along her thigh, and the heat radiating from his body was lapping away at her every worry. His hands wandered everywhere, touching, testing, exciting her. Oh, how she wanted him.

She understood sex for sex's sake and wanted to be with Sam no matter what his desire was right this instant. There wasn't a single doubt in her mind that she wanted sex with Sam. Yet their coming together, wrapping, entangling, growing closer and closer still, seemed very different in comparison with others.

Sam rolled her, his weight pressing her down. She rocked against his strong thighs as he held her arms above her head with one hand and devoured her breasts with his mouth and tongue. Fireworks seemed to skip across her chest and burrow deep toward her core. She needed him. Soon, completely under his spell, she was lost to any thoughts beyond flesh and sensations, and the burning desire for him and him alone. With every cell in her body ignited from his touch, she bucked against him, opening, nearly begging for him to put an end to her frustration. She needed him inside. Needed to connect in the deepest way possible with him.

She held on to his hips, felt the muscular bulge of his ass as he followed her lead to the bedside table, sheathed himself, then slowly entered her. He'd already worked her into a frenzy and her moisture made their introduction smooth and, if possible, even more stimulating. The fresh sensations zinging throughout her pelvis made her gasp.

"Are you okay?" he quickly responded.

"Oh, God, yes. Don't stop."

He did stop, just long enough to deliver a broad, I'm-in-control smile. A shaft of moonlight caught that wicked twinkle in his eyes as he planted one big hand on her hip and began thrusting and withdrawing, never breaking their staring match. Wanting to close her eyes and crawl inside, to curl up with all the amazing feelings coursing through her body, she forced her gaze to stay locked with his, mainly because he willed it. And it both frightened and excited her to see the near wild look of passion on his face. He'd given in totally to their one point of connection—him being inside her—and his obvious desire to satisfy her.

Did it feel as astonishing to him as it did to her? His long, smooth thrusts seemed to pass over every single nerve ending. He treated her to minutes and minutes and more minutes at this heightened, sensitive place. Someday she would have to thank him profusely, but not now. Right now all she could do was experience everything he gave her. Her arms tensed, hands grasping the bedsheets, and she screwed her eyes tight as her mind drifted toward bliss. Then he pushed faster. Harder. The sensations tensing, tangling and balling up, building deeper, wider, threatening to overwhelm her. She held on to him with all of her might. Her gasps came quicker. She clamped her thighs tighter around his hips and lifted her pelvis just so, adding pressure and, oh, yes, yes, yes, pleasure, pleasure beyond her wildest hopes.

"Don't stop." Her voice sounded strangely disconnected from her body. Their body. Because they were a single unit now.

Sam didn't stop. He built and built and finally came at her with everything he had.

She sucked in air, held it, and as he drove at record speed into the center of her universe she caught fire one spark at a time. A twitch, a rush of tingles breaking out from the hot gathering knot that grew and demanded release. Soon. Soon deep, breathtaking spasms exploded inside her, overtaking her, shooting down her legs and up to her breasts, holding her in suspension of time and mind. Out of control, her back and neck arched as he continued to push into her, prolonging her rush of blinding feelings.

Everything burst apart, flattening her, as a low, distant groan grew, building somewhere out there in the world she'd just left behind. Somehow, Sam moved even harder and his groan changed to a grunting as he thrust and pumped on and on until he joined her on the other side of their bliss.

Like rag dolls they landed in a clump of body parts on her mattress, sated and stunned by each other. Snuggling into the crook of his strong and inviting arm, feeling as she never had before, safe and completely claimed, she sighed and shut her eyes. No words needed to be said.

With only the occasional croak of a frog on the lawn, she drank in the contentment and silence, and the faint yet steady stroke of Sam's fingers along her arm. Then, knowing for this single moment all was perfect in her world, and as if she was having an out-of-body experience, she gently floated off to sleep.

Morning came entirely too quickly. Andrea cracked open one eye to find Sam blissfully asleep beside her. She began the slow process of stretching and slowly rejoining the living when crying woke her up. Dani!

She'd completely forgotten about the boy.

She shook Sam awake. "Dani's crying. Maybe you should get him."

Without a word, the once big puddle of flesh beside her came right to attention. Though he didn't look in the least bit sure of where he was just yet. He jumped out of the bed, searched for his clothes and hopped into first one leg then the other of his suit slacks, then strode out of the room, from the looks of him not anywhere near awake. "Coming, Dani. Hold on."

Being a single father, he'd probably gotten down the routine of waking up at a moment's notice to a science.

Andrea smiled. She lay there, drinking in the morning and the lovely body aches from last night's gymnastics with Sam, and the delicious lingering sensations between her thighs, thinking how lucky she was to have met him. Then one negative thought grabbed her by the throat.

Having him meant having Dani. How could she have forgotten about Dani so easily? Which made her wonder if she was ready to be a girlfriend to a guy who was still getting used to being a single father. Was that even what he wanted from her? If they got involved, would she be a girlfriend or a mother figure for Dani? What was Sam looking for?

The complications made her head spin, so she got out of bed to help ignore them, and made a quick bathroom stop before reporting for breakfast duty.

Sam helped Dani get dressed, then took the boy to the bathroom. Sitting him on the small tiled vanity counter, he washed his face.

"Why I sleep here, Dad?"

"I had to work late, so Andrea let you sleep over."

"I like *my* bed."

Point taken! "I know, Dani, and tonight you'll sleep there. Are you hungry?"

The boy nodded.

"Then let's see what we can rustle up for breakfast." He held Dani's hand and they walked down the short hall to the kitchen. Already he could smell coffee brewing and toast. The thought of seeing Andrea in the daylight, after ravishing her last night, excited him, yet he wondered how she'd receive him now. He hoped she wouldn't go shy or make things awkward, because from his standpoint things were going great. "Hey, good morning." He went the casual, oh-yeah-I-sleep-over-with-my-son-all-the-time routine.

"Hi!" Her eyes, without a trace of makeup, looked younger, oddly enough, bigger and browner, too. He'd noticed last night in the moonlight she hadn't had makeup on, but he'd been too distracted to comment. Very distracted, and gratefully so. "You two hungry?"

"Yeah!" said Dani.

"I've got plenty of eggs. Why not omelets?"

"I want cereal," Dani said.

"I think I have some of that," she said, opening a cupboard and pulling out a box. Sam could plainly see she was ready to cook more eggs.

"If you don't mind, I'll take you up on those eggs," he said.

"Done." She glanced over her shoulder and when their gazes connected a zing through his center served as a great wake-up call.

He could easily get used to looking at her in the morning. "Sorry I fell asleep too soon to enjoy your cheese omelet last night."

She found a small bowl and poured in a big helping of multigrain cereal for Dani. "I'll consider last night my practice session," she said, the double entendre making Andrea and Sam lock eyes again in a totally adult way. If what they'd shared had been practice, he couldn't wait for the dress rehearsal. "So you want more?"

Oh, yes, he wanted more of her. Hopefully soon. "Loaded question." She gave a quick, breathy laugh. "Yes. Definitely. I'll have—" he placed his hand around her upper arm and squeezed it the tiniest bit "—more."

She gave a coy smile as she looked up at him, and he bent and kissed her good morning. "Thank you," he whispered. "For a thousand things."

Her eyes widened the tiniest bit. "You're welcome, and thank you, too," she said, her gaze shifting downward and her cheeks turning pink before she got back to the business of pouring milk over Dani's cereal and whipping eggs for Sam's fresh omelet.

What did all this mean? He'd found a woman he liked.

A lot. Had finally had sex with her. Which had been great. Beyond great. Of course he wanted to see her again. Often. But he was a busy doctor, a new and adjusting father. Were there hours enough in the day for all the time she deserved, too? Or was he already thinking up reasons to keep a distance between them? The safe route?

His phone rang. He quickly checked to see if it was the ICU. No. It was Bob Brinker, the lead on his missions team. "Do you mind if I get this?"

She puckered that sexy mouth of hers and shook her head, distracted and busy with making the omelet.

He'd missed the call but Bob had left a long message. They'd rescheduled the meeting Sam had missed last week for tonight. Did it work for him?

Hell, did it? He'd missed putting Dani to bed last night. Then Sam read the last sentence. *It's the only night all of us are available.* How could he refuse?

He scrunched up his face and looked at Andrea. "I hate to ask you this, but could you possibly watch Dani for me at my place tonight? They've rescheduled the missions meeting. It's the only night that works for the rest of them."

She glanced cautiously toward Dani, then back at him. "If you don't have a choice but to go, then okay."

Did he have a choice? He really needed to rethink his priorities. He'd committed to this mission long before Dani's adoption had become final. Hell, if it hadn't been for his medical mission trips, he'd never have met Dani in the first place.

But things were different now. He was a father with a son who needed him as much as possible, and he'd just met Andrea, was already crazy about her and wanted to know her more. Juggling his job, fatherhood plus a new romance was complicated. Maybe Katie had been right— he wanted too much.

He looked at Dani. No way had Katie been right about

not adopting. Dani was the best part of his life. Then he glanced at Andrea, putting a perfectly fluffy cheese omelet onto a plate especially for him. A lady who didn't cook had just given him the best she had, not to mention what she'd given him last night, and that meant something

Who knew where the best of Andrea Rimmer might lead? One thing was sure, if they were going to pursue this "thing" going on between them, she deserved the best of him, too.

He pushed Dial on his phone. "Hey, Bob? Yeah, I got hung up in ICU last night. Never made it home. So, listen, I'm going to have to ask you to fill me in on whatever goes on tonight. I need to be home with my boy tonight."

A subtle smile crossed Andrea's lips as she handed him his breakfast, then their eyes met when she gave him a fork, and he knew he'd made the right decision.

A week later...

It was a big day. Sam had cut short his afternoon appointment schedule by two so he could personally take Dani to get his official prosthetic eye. Andrea had made a big deal about not showing it to him until it was inside the boy's eye socket, and who was he to argue?

They'd spent a couple more nights together over the past week, one planned and one, unfortunately, another last-minute "Can you watch Dani for me so I can attend the early morning staff meeting?" Turned out having someone to be there for Dani in the morning for breakfast and to get him ready for Aunt Cat's was a win-win situation. Andrea had opted to sleep over the night before, rather than get up at the crack of dawn and fight the traffic over to his house.

Any night making love with Andrea was a win-win,

even though he felt tension mounting over the fact he'd yet to be completely honest with her.

He guided Dani toward the elevator. "After this appointment, you won't have to wear that darned patch anymore."

"Yay." Dani clapped his pudgy hands.

Sam's stomach felt a little queasy as he worried about how the prosthetic would fit and, almost more important, look. Would it be obvious that it was a fake eye? What if he didn't like Andrea's version of Dani's iris?

He took a deep breath and got into the elevator, choosing to focus on more positive things, like how incredibly great it was to make love with Andrea, and to spend time with her. But where did they go from here? If he wanted an honest relationship, he'd have to come clean. He'd let her think he was from a big family—which theoretically he was in one sense—when he was actually the kid of a young single mother who hadn't had a clue how to be a mom or how to support both of them with the few skills she'd learned with only a high school education. She'd had to work two jobs, and Sam had had to spend nights alone in a shabby apartment, afraid and vulnerable, until he was ten and the courts had taken him away from his mother. And she'd let him go.

Soon enough they were in the basement, and knowing the routine Dani ran ahead. "Hey, hold on there, buddy, you don't want to wind up in the wrong place." He avoided saying "In the morgue."

"I want to see Andrea!" Dani eagerly kept going, knowing the way from all his prior appointments, so Sam picked up his pace to catch up.

"Okay, but let's go in together." He took his hand just in time to open the O&A department door, wondering why the dark, dingy hallway and office in the corner didn't creep out the kid.

Judith Rimmer met them in the display room, wearing the headgear getup and smiling. "It's your big day, Dani. Let me get Andrea," she said to Sam.

Almost immediately, Andrea emerged from the workshop, wearing a lab coat and a huge smile. "I wanted to give your eye one last polish," she said to Dani, as if preparing to give the boy a special gem. "Want to watch?"

Andrea had explained the entire process to Sam, and the final step was to cover the prosthetic in clear resin, and to polish the living daylights out of the new eye.

Being only three, Sam wasn't sure how much Dani understood about everything that was going on, but the kid couldn't look any more excited or expectant than if it was his birthday. "Yes!" Dani ran to follow Andrea into the back and the workshop. Sam chatted with Judith to pass the time. Soon enough Dani and Andrea reappeared.

Andrea helped Dani sit on a chair with a booster seat near the eye display counter. "Let's take off this patch." She gently removed it, and Dani watched and smiled the whole time. So trusting.

She checked the alignment of his new eye, had him open and close his eyes several times. She even checked for natural secretions and anatomical function before giving it her final seal of approval. Dani sat perfectly still like a little soldier the whole time.

Truth was, Andrea was a natural with his son. Her gentle touch, her care and concern for Dani, the way he trusted her. All systems seemed to say go, yet his lousy experience with Katie held him back from taking things further between them. Hadn't that proved he didn't know how to really love someone? He'd been completely convinced Katie had been the one for him, had been for all the years they'd dated, yet when he'd finally got around to asking her to marry him, her career had suddenly come first. How wrong could a guy be? What did it say for his judgment where women were concerned? Now he had a son who needed to come first. Sam knew firsthand that the less drama in life, the better stability for the kid. Wasn't that what the person who had really become his mother, not just a foster caregiver, had taught him? Since Mom Murphy had died, the person he'd trusted more than anyone, he'd struggled to let anyone get close. Hell, Katie could attest to that. Did Andrea deserve the same treatment?

Plus Andrea had been candid with Sam in one of their post-lovemaking talks. She longed to be the artist she'd set out to be at university, and felt for the past four years her dreams had been on hold while she'd apprenticed in ocularistry. Yet she obviously loved her clients at the hospital and enjoyed the work—Dani being a case in point— which proved she was as confused as he was. But had she been trying to warn him? Was she still holding out for her big break, the same way Katie had been?

He stepped out of his thoughts in time to see Dani turning around with his prosthetic eye in place. Sam had to do a double take to remember which eye was real and which was fake. Holy cow, she'd replicated his real eye perfectly. A mirror image. So much so, it brought a lump to his throat. "That looks fantastic, buddy." His grateful gaze met Andrea's. She looked relieved.

But Dani seemed puzzled, and usually when he did he asked Sam a question. This time, though, he turned to Andrea. "I can't see." He covered his good eye to make sure.

Sam's throat lump doubled. How the hell was he supposed to explain the truth?

Andrea went down on her knees to be at eye level with Dani. She cupped his shoulders and gave the sincerest look he'd ever seen. "Honey, the eyes we make here can't see. You'll always have to rely on this one." She touched him above his right eye. "This one will be good enough for both your eyes. This one—" she touched his brow above the new prosthetic "—is just to look pretty, so you don't have to wear that patch. Is that all right?"

Dani nodded solemnly. "I guess so."

Sam stepped closer, first giving Andrea an appreciative glance and nod, then studying his son's new eye up close. "It's amazing how perfectly matched this is to his own eye." He hugged Dani and looked at Andrea. "I can't thank you enough for making the most incredible prosthetic. Only a true artist could duplicate his iris so perfectly. My God. I'm shocked at how great it is." Maybe he was laying it on too thick, but he meant every word and gratitude got the better of him. "You really are a great artist."

"Now I think you're going overboard."

He touched her arm. "No. I'm not. This is fantastic. No one will know this isn't his real eye without looking really closely. You've just given him an amazing gift."

"It's my job."

"And you were made for it." From the other side of the room, Judith spoke up.

Sam could see a flash of rebellion in Andrea's reaction over the reminder from her grandmother of that continual war between practical day job and the artist itching to take flight. She chose not to say anything just then.

Dani jumped down from his chair and walked to a mirror, studying his image really closely. He made monkey faces and joked around, but Sam knew he liked what he saw. As for Sam, he couldn't be happier. His son wouldn't need to ever feel inferior, wearing a perfect eye like this one.

Andrea stepped up behind Dani, placed her fingertips on his narrow shoulders and spoke to him in the mirror. "You shouldn't fiddle with your new eye or treat it like a toy. If it bothers you or feels uncomfortable, you ask Daddy to bring you to me so we can polish it." She turned to Sam, her expression clouding with something unnamed, and she avoided making eye contact, instead seeming to look at his shoulder. "You'll need to clean it a couple times a day at first so it doesn't get gummy. Until his eye socket gets used to it."

"Will do. Are you all right?"

Her lower lip quivered the tiniest bit. "Yeah." She nodded, tried to brush off the emotions obviously building inside, doing anything rather than look him straight on.

Judith, as though sensing something was up, took Dani by the hand. "Would you like to see where I make eyes?" she said, leading the boy toward the workshop.

"Is that a hat?" Dani commented about her headgear, then took her hand, eager to follow her to the "eye" room.

"It makes things look really big. Want to look through it?"

"Yes!"

Once they were gone, Sam reached for Andrea and kissed her. "What's wrong?" He held her close, biting back his own mixed-up feelings, reliving all the reasons Dani had needed the prosthetic in the first place.

She shook her head against his shoulder. "Remember that first night I came to your house and you told me your biggest fear was the thought of Dani losing his other eye?"

He held her closer, kissed the top of her head. "Yes. It still is."

"I worry about that, too. I've fallen in love with your son and I can't stand the thought of him suffering or losing any more than he already has."

The lump in Sam's throat became too big to swallow so he couldn't speak. But he held on to Andrea with all his strength, hoping that maybe the two of them together could will away any future problems for Dani, even while knowing they were powerless. Life happened. It just did. There was no good-luck charm to ward off bad events or illnesses, or parents letting their kids go into foster care, no way to skip around the messy parts. What would be would be for Dani, and they'd have to deal with whatever played out. Andrea's support meant the world to him, helped him think he could get through whatever lay ahead.

As they stood holding each other it hit Sam how, without even realizing it, they'd become a kind of family where Dani was concerned. Yet he hadn't even gotten up the guts to tell Andrea the truth, and if he couldn't do that, how could he ever love her? Did he love her? Wasn't that how he'd started off with Katie, jumping right in up to his neck, deciding she was the perfect girl for him, only to find out several years later she had been anything but that girl. Even if he did think he might love Andrea, being a reasonable man he still couldn't believe that was possible yet, so was he ready to tell her something he wasn't even sure he was capable of?

Plus he had Dani now. There would be two broken hearts if things didn't work out. Yet Dani had fallen for Andrea right off, and kids were usually pretty good judges of character. Which brought his thoughts full circle back to Andrea, the woman in his arms who'd gone all weepy worrying about his son. Yeah, they'd become a modern-day melded family, whether they were ready for it or not.

Those astounding thoughts had him squeezing her even tighter, mostly for support. How had this happened so quickly, and was it even possible?

CHAPTER SIX

SAM HAD TALKED Andrea into joining him and Dani at the park closest to St. Francis of the Valley Hospital after the appointment. Still being spring, the sun was far from setting at 6:00 p.m. "Let's celebrate Dani's new eye," Sam had said.

Since she'd made it, how could she refuse?

Earlier Andrea had been hit with a world of worries about Dani. Sam had spoken of his fear the first night she'd gone to his house—that his son might lose his other eye. The thought made her feel queasy. It was also a sure sign she'd fallen for the kid. And his dad. How could her life get tipped on its ear in a month?

Maybe she should have put more thought into dating a man with a kid, a man with a huge family photo on his wall and a framed parable about saving starfish one at a time. None of which she could relate to and, honestly, was afraid she'd never be able to. But it was too late now to worry about "getting it" where Sam and his dreams and desires were concerned. She was already crazy about both of them.

Sam sat beside her on the bench in his work suit, a beige one with an Easter-egg-yellow shirt and, in typical Dr. Sammy style, a SpongeBob tie for the kids at the hospital. His legs were extended and crossed at the ankles, arms stretched wide along the back of the bench. Confident and relaxed. Instead of relaxing, like him, she perched on the edge of the bench, ready to run after Dani at a moment's notice in case he needed her on the kiddie slide or mini jungle gym. Sam was all about giving the kid independence. She was about keeping him safe.

A grin stretched across Dani's bright face. He teetered, then stood at the bottom of the slide before he galloped for the swings. Andrea hopped up and met him just in time to set him inside the toddler bucket-styled swing. That grin disappeared and he shook his head, pointing to the standard swings, the big-kid swings, down the line on the thick metal play set frame.

Andrea glanced at Sam, who was already up and heading their way. With a kind smile he lifted his son like a sack of potatoes over his hip, which Dani loved, then walked him down to an empty regular swing seat and put him in the center.

"You've got to hold on really tight," he said, making sure the boy's hands held the swing chain securely on both sides. Dani gave a solemn nod, as if realizing this was a big step in his playground life. A step worthy of his new eye.

She'd made plenty of eyes for patients during her nearly four-year apprenticeship, and she'd witnessed firsthand how life-changing that could be for them, which was incredibly satisfying. But with Dani—she patted one forearm, then the other—never before had the gratification been so intense that it raised the hair on her arms.

A few moments went by with only the sound of Dani's delighted squeals while Sam gently pushed him on the swing. Andrea stood enjoying the view and the light evening breeze, warmth pulsing in her heart. Beyond the huge sandbox area with all the playground apparatus, the grass was fragrant, freshly mown, spring green and dotted with young myrtles and ash trees. In a decade they'd offer shade in this newly opened park. For now, they were simply new and pretty to look at.

The vision inspired her, making her want to capture the essence of this moment with bright colors on a canvas. Thoughts swirled through her brain. Creative sparks made her come alive in a way she hadn't for months. On the verge of telling Sam she had to get right home, he looked up with an earnest expression, a man completely content pushing his kid on a swing, as if something had just occurred to him, too.

He started talking, but she was so lost in her thoughts she didn't hear him until she picked up at the point of new shoes. "What?"

"I said, when my mom used to take all of us for new shoes the week before school started, when we got home we'd all try them on and parade around for Dad. And Dad would say, 'It's a good day. All my kids have new shoes. Let's go have ice cream.'" He looked at her nostalgically over Dani on the swing, capturing her gaze. "Well, it's not just a good day today, it's a great day. Thanks to you, my boy has a beautiful new eye. What do you say we go get ice cream?"

Dani cheered, and there was no way right then Andrea could make an excuse to go home to paint.

That night, right after they'd put Dani to bed, they made love, then cuddled in Sam's huge bed. Sam surprised Andrea and opened up, telling her the entire story of how he'd come to be Dani's father. He shared every detail, including the heartbreak of Katie walking away over his decision, and it brought tears to Andrea's eyes.

Their relationship had grown so quickly, it seemed, and his willingness to share feelings normally left close to the heart was part of the reason. She thought how they'd both tiptoed into this new relationship, and she didn't want to upset the fragile foundation forming between them with one ongoing concern that he might want to be with her only because he needed a mother for his son. So she kept it to herself and they made love again.

Now stretched out side by side, they held hands and stared at the ceiling, letting the flush of fresh lovemaking spend its remaining moments covering them before dissolving into the dark.

Earlier Sam had asked her if she could watch Dani on Thursday night while he filled in for another doctor friend who needed to attend his son's sports banquet. After sidestepping the subject with sex, she couldn't, in the name of honesty, avoid any longer telling him what was on her mind.

Andrea first snuggled against his chest, which was lightly dusted with crinkly brown hair, thinking she'd never get tired of how sturdy he felt or his natural guy scent, and wondering over the difference in their skin tones. Then she broached the tough topic by sitting up and engaging Sam's full attention. Except his attention settled solely on her breasts, so she wrapped the sheet around her chest.

"You know how I love Dani," she said. He nodded. "And frankly you've given me lots of chances to get to know him. The thing is, I've been putting off painting a lot lately and I'm beginning to panic about it."

That got his full attention. He seemed uncomfortable, realizing he was keeping her from her passion. "The last thing I want to do is stand in the way of your painting."

She leaned forward. "I believe you, and I have to admit it's always fun to watch Dani, but…"

He went up on his elbow. "Well, that's something, then, right? Because he loves you so much, and I trust you, I always know he's in good hands with you. And that means a lot to me."

"I'm glad you trust me, but it's clear you're the center of that boy's universe. He loves you so much and wants to be with *you*."

"Thanks. I know, but you two are really great together, too. You've got a very special friendship going on."

"So much so I'm beginning to wonder if this is what motherhood feels like, which scares the daylights out of me." She'd decided to tiptoe into the conversation.

He grabbed her and pulled her close. "Aw, you're just being a scaredy-cat about kids." Sounding like a typical pediatrician. "You're a natural."

A natural? Being raised by a deeply depressed mother and an oblivious father probably made her the furthest thing from that.

"Don't get me wrong," she said, glancing up at his chin, memorizing the fine stubble there. "I adore Dani, but he's your son and you need to be there for him as much as you possibly can."

"I am there for him, every day. I get him up every morning and put him to bed most nights. He knows I'm his dad, and I love being his dad." He squeezed her shoulder. "I even hope to have more children, too. I guess I should be up front with you about that, right?"

Now he tells her? She sat up again. "Yes, you definitely should."

Why did his hope for a big family make her immediately wonder where she'd fit in? He wanted more children? What exactly did he have in mind?

"Sam, you're a great dad, Dani is thriving living with you. But lately I feel like I'm doing as much, if not more, of the caregiving as you." She wouldn't dare mention that it also felt like being second best to his job, just as it'd always felt with her father. But it did!

"My job will always keep me busy, it's the nature of the beast. I *will*, however, get a babysitter before the end of this week. I promise." He looked sincere as all get-out, and she felt obligated to believe him.

"Thank you." It wasn't a perfect solution, but at least Dani could go to sleep in his own bed and she wouldn't be the one always putting him there. They kissed more, but she couldn't get into it. "You seriously want more kids?"

"Yes, but not, like, tomorrow. I come from a big family and I want the same. I've told you that."

Something about his answer didn't ring true, but she couldn't quite put her finger on it. Where did his need and desire to have a big family leave her? If they were together, would she have a say in the matter? This conversation was making her feel like a helpless child all over again. "But doesn't it take two?" Actually, he'd already gotten around that loophole by adopting. Would he do it again? Her head throbbed with questions.

"I'm not rushing things," he said. "I'm just being honest."

This obviously meant he was serious about her, and on so many levels she was crazy about him, too, but she couldn't discount her ambivalence about his desire for a big family. Not with her background.

Maybe he deserved to hear her side of the story. She owed it to him. "I know how it feels, as a kid, to always want my dad home, because he never was. That's probably why I'm so sensitive to that for Dani. But unlike you with Dani, when my dad was home he'd be completely distracted with work. I'd be, like, 'Daddy, look what I drew,' and he'd glance up from his paperwork and say, 'Not now.' Sometimes I'd be quiet like a good little girl and wait for him, but I felt as though he didn't even know I was in the same room."

Sam pulled her closer, wrapping her in his arms. "You deserved better than that." He kissed the top of her head.

"I'm not asking for sympathy, I'm just saying that kind of experience doesn't make for 'natural' skills in parenting, like you've experienced."

He went still for a heartbeat, then sighed. "Trust me, if I can do it, you can do it."

Maybe she should be flattered that he felt open enough to tell her his plans, but she had plans, too. And she needed to think about those plans as well, but he pulled her back toward him. They snuggled down again and kissed a few more times. Her mind drifted to other points of anxiety in her life—ignoring her art, her love-hate relationship with her job, loving the patients but not the administrative part and feeling pushed to run a department. She stopped the kiss in the middle.

"My grandmother's retirement is getting closer and closer and soon, if I don't figure something out, they'll expect me to be the head of the department, which means administrative meetings and more responsibility. Where will that leave my painting? Honestly, I'm feeling trapped."

"Is this your father's or grandmother's idea?"

"Both, but mostly my father's."

"Then tell him you don't want that responsibility. Tell him you want to go back to working part-time so you can still pursue your painting."

It sounded so logical, but Sam didn't know her father as she knew her father. "It's not that easy."

He didn't push her on the topic. Maybe he sensed what she knew firsthand, that there was no saying no to Jerome Rimmer.

He went quiet for a second. "Do I make you feel trapped?"

"No." She lifted her head to make eye contact. "No.

But I can't be your babysitter, Sam, or a stand-in parent for Dani."

"That's the last thing I want."

"If we become a couple, I don't want to feel second in line to your job, because that's how I always felt with my dad. Nor do I ever want Dani to feel that way."

"I understand. That's the last thing in the world I'd want, either. And I really don't want to interfere with your art." He held her close, ran his fingers over her hair. "We'll work something out. I just need some time to think about this."

Right, men were task-oriented problem solvers. But this wasn't an easy-to-solve situation. She didn't have a clue what he'd come up with, but right now she was exhausted and couldn't summon a thought about what she should do, so she let him hold her, satisfied she'd said her piece. She'd let him know her fears, and why she was the way she was, totally ambivalent about his big family plans, and he'd accepted her concerns. But the most important thing of all was that they'd come closer as a couple tonight.

They'd taken their worries and fears and acted on them with caveman sex just now, the one thing they seemed to do best together. At least from Sam's view it was the least complicated part of their relationship. Plus it fit right in with his lifelong habit of trying to prove himself worth keeping. He knew how to make her lose it, and did it as often as he could.

He wasn't using her. He respected her completely, and he loved how she got along with his son. He could see a future for them, but they'd only started dating. Maybe it had been a boneheaded idea to announce how he wanted a big family. He was lucky she hadn't run for the hills.

It was his time-to-be-honest moment, and since Andrea had drifted off to sleep, he couldn't avoid thinking about it. He wanted to be around her as much as possible. They both led complicated lives, and he felt guilty keeping her from her painting. He understood her inner battle about always having to create time for her passion, as if it didn't mean as much as the more practical job of making a decent living while helping others. Maybe he could come up with a way that she could do both?

What if he asked her to move in with them?

If she did, she could paint every evening if she wanted to. He admired her talent, wanted nothing more than for her to feel fulfilled. He and Dani would learn to respect and honor her need to paint and stay out of her way when she did. He had a perfectly available spare bedroom he could turn into a studio for her, too.

Okay, his solution sounded more practical than romantic, and also scared the daylights out of him. Maybe he should think more about this first before he brought it up. But he had to be honest with himself.

I want her here. I see a future with her. I... I think I love her.

He shook his head, suddenly needing to take an extra breath. He did. He loved her. But she was all tangled up with job changes and a demanding father, not a great time for a woman to fall in love. And how could he tell her he loved her when he hadn't been completely honest with her about his family, and how he'd been the foster kid left alone until the Murphys had taken him in? When would he quit feeling unworthy of being loved because his mother had walked away from him? Wasn't he in charge of his life now? So why couldn't he come clean with Andrea and tell her he'd been an only child like her, and in two completely different ways they had both been abandoned.

Because it still hurt too much, and he didn't want her sympathy. He'd proved himself by becoming a successful doctor, yet why did he still feel unworthy of a woman's love?

It hurt too much to let the old pushed-down feelings out, so he focused back on Andrea and her issues. She needed to figure out how to deal with her father. It would be a shame if his overbearing attitude chased Andrea out of the profession. The way she'd painted Dani's iris was uncanny. No digital computer program could duplicate what she'd captured with her artistic eye. What she'd done for Dani was nothing short of a miracle. Just like that eye peeking through the keyhole painting. People were her canvases, and didn't the saying go that the eye was the mirror to the soul? What she did on the job was nothing short of art. Andrea had a gift that needed to be shared with the world, whether on canvas or with glass eyes and silicone ears.

There had to be some way he could help her. Should he confront her father for her? No, that was her business, but it ticked him off that Jerome made Andrea's life so difficult.

Now his head was spinning a mile a minute. He wanted to solve her problem because he truly cared about her. He knew he couldn't resolve her issues, that it was totally up to her to work it out with her father. But wasn't the hospital redoing the lobby? Wouldn't they be looking for new artwork once they remodeled?

Those big splashy paintings on the walls at her house would be the perfect style for a modern hospital. Who did he need to talk to about that?

Then the one painting in particular that stood out from all the others at her house came to mind, the single eye peeking through a door keyhole. In his opinion, it was a masterpiece, and no doubt featured the skill she'd developed in her apprenticeship as an ocularist. The iris. The mirror to the soul. And the world was filled with billions of people with their own individual versions.

She'd never run out of subjects to paint.

Sleep would probably never come tonight. He'd at least diverted his thoughts from old painful ones to Andrea's concerns. He smiled with satisfaction into the dark because he'd found a way for Andrea to share her talent with the world. At the hospital. Genius!

Now all he had to do was convince her to face her father and tell him to back off, to let her do her job the way she wanted, the way things were right now. Being a department head might hold prestige for Dr. Rimmer, but Andrea was a modern woman, why couldn't she have it all on her terms? Not everyone was meant to be a department administrator. She had an artist's soul.

CHAPTER SEVEN

TELEVISION NEWS WAS playing the minute Sam and Andrea hit the hospital lobby the next morning. The huge flat screen on the farthest wall ran pictures of death and destruction in Mexico, with captions. A drug cartel had bombed several places, one being the village where one of the drug traffickers who'd cooperated with the police lived. As usual, the innocents had paid the price.

The explosions and subsequent fires had taken hundreds of lives and caused countless injuries across the countryside, leaving only rubble and near total devastation in one quiet border village between Mexico and the United States. The hospitals were overflowing and emergency personnel stretched beyond their limits. The area needed help, and even the Red Cross didn't seem to be enough.

Andrea stood with her mouth open, reading the horrible story. Sam put his arm around her for comfort and it occurred to him that was the first time he'd made a public display of his affection for her at the hospital. Despite the horrible news, the comforting part felt good.

"Hey, Dr. Marcus," a passing young resident said. "Terrible stuff, right?"

"Unbelievable. So senseless," he replied, still trying to get his head around the incident.

"A few of us are making plans to head down to Mexicali this weekend to help out. Someone needs to triage those patients in Cuernavaca. Is your passport up to date?"

"Of course."

"Why don't you come, too?"

Sam glanced at Andrea, who wore an uncertain expression, and he held off accepting, saying he'd think about it.

The resident seemed gung ho on helping, and recognizing Andrea he continued, "Aren't you from the anaplastology department? You should go, too," he said to her. "The explosion and fire probably left a lot of people with facial injuries. There might be all kinds of ways you could help."

This young, long-haired resident's enthusiasm was almost palpable, and compelling, and it was quickly rubbing off on Sam.

"I, uh…" Andrea seemed stumped by his challenge.

Sam stepped in. "We'll definitely think about it and get back to you, Anthony. When are you planning to leave?"

"Tomorrow, 6:00 a.m. The sooner we get there, the better. The border town is only about four hours away— we've already arranged for four free vans from the local car dealership." He said that part to Andrea, as if it might help her make up her mind. "And we plan to come back late Sunday. We're trying to get the hospital to donate supplies, too. We're still working out the details, but I'll definitely get back to you later."

As it was Friday morning, the new doctor had a lot to work out in a very short time, but judging by his exuberance, and seeing a little bit of himself in the guy, Sam had no doubt all would be arranged in record time.

"Yeah, give me a call," Sam said, putting his hand at the small of the back of the mildly stunned lady beside him to guide her toward the elevator. They didn't say a thing about the medical mission plans as they walked. Once at the elevators, where he needed to go up and she down, he pecked her on the cheek, liking the freedom of letting the world know—well, the hospital, anyway—that he and Andrea were a definite item.

"I'll see you later," he said, enjoying the subtle twinkle in her eyes after the kiss. She must've liked his public display of affection, too. "Oh, by the way, *is* your passport up to date?" he asked, just before stepping into a nearly full elevator.

Her eyes widened and she gave a closed-mouth huff in reply.

If Sam expected her to drop everything, pack up and head south at a moment's notice, he'd better think again. Though she had to admit that for one split second she'd found the offer intriguing. Frustrated about being put on the spot, she got in the next elevator going down.

What about Dani? Sam might not be married, but he wasn't a single guy anymore. He couldn't just drop everything and travel to parts unknown. He had a son to think of. If she did go, and there was a big "if" about that, who'd look after Dani? The mere fact that Dani was always her first concern made her stop and think. She was already in over her head with the Marcus men.

The elevator door closed. She was the only person heading to the basement.

More truth, who was she to judge how Sam and Cat bartered time and money? The lady cared deeply for Dani. Andrea had seen it with her own eyes whenever Cat had brought Dani in for his appointments, and she probably loved having him around her boys, as well. He was such a sweetie.

She got out of the elevator and headed down the dreary green and beige linoleum hallway toward her department.

Andrea had to admit, until she decided whether to go or

stay, whatever Sam worked out in order to take this last-minute medical mission trip was between Cat and Sam.

What she needed to do was search her soul about whether to go or not. The thought made a band tighten around her head.

Andrea opened the door, checking her watch. Her first appointment was in ten minutes and she needed to get the custom prosthesis ready for attachment. She rushed around, gathering everything she'd need when the patient entered the department.

From his records she knew he was a veteran who'd survived two tours in Afghanistan, only to return home and get his ear bitten off by a neighbor's Rottweiler. From personal experience, he was an affable guy who just wanted to look normal again. Surgical reconstruction had been ruled out because the damage was too great, so he'd been coming to Andrea for custom prosthetic restoration. He'd decided against surgical magnet placement and instead had undergone a small but important bone anchor procedure, which allowed her to create a bar-clip attachment for the perfectly duplicated mirror-image ear, if she did say so herself.

Greg smiled widely, his ball cap tilting low over what was left of his right ear, hiding the fact he didn't have one. She greeted him, and after a little small talk about how his surgery had gone, she revealed the silicone ear she'd made to match his skin tone and the existing ear.

"Wow, this looks weird but great," he said. "I'll be two-eared again." He chuckled.

"You won't be lopsided anymore," she said, motioning for him to sit as she adjusted the lights for best visibility. She'd spent several hours replicating his other ear first with sketches, then in a mold, then touching it up to be a nearly perfect mirror-image match to the other side, but in silicone. "That's new." She always got a kick out of his tattoo sleeves, noticing he'd added a new colorful section just above his wrist on one forearm.

"Yeah, I saw the porpoise and thought it'd be cool there."

While they chitchatted she removed the large flat bandage covering the implanted bar and easily clipped the new ear in place, adjusting the tilt to match the other side. "See how easy this is? Now you try." She removed the ear and handed it to him.

Under her tutelage, he attached his new ear, then sat and stared at himself in the mirror for several seconds, turning first this way, then that. "Wow. It looks real."

"Of course it looks real." She couldn't deny the pride she always felt when clients were happy with what she'd made for them. "It should help your hearing by twenty percent, too. Those auricles are there for a reason, you know."

"Look at this!" He put his ball cap back on his short-cropped military-style hair, and it was now perfectly balanced between two ears.

"You look great." Her smile was genuine and heartfelt. "But, to be honest, I kind of like the tilted cap look, too."

"Thanks, Andrea." The sincerity pouring out of his gaze nearly melted her.

"You're welcome, Greg. Come back anytime you think you need an adjustment, okay?"

"You got it."

Next she had an appointment in the hospital to measure a young woman who'd lost most of her nose to cancer. Andrea had been studying the woman's photographs and wondered, since now was a perfect opportunity, if the patient might want a sexy new nose, or if she'd rather stick with a replica of what she'd been born with. It could be a touchy subject, and Andrea was working out in her head how she wanted to broach the topic when a text message came through.

Lunch?

She knew exactly who it was and texted back.

What time?

After she'd finished her bedside appointment, having discovered that the young lady would indeed love a new nose, specifically one like Reese Witherspoon's—which put a smile on Andrea's face—she met up with Sam in the hospital cafeteria, excited about her next project but even more excited about seeing him.

Then she ran into her father. "Andrea, you're just the person I wanted to see."

"Hi, Dad." Why did she always go on alert whenever he spoke to her? "You know Sam Marcus, right?"

Her father glanced distractedly at Sam, only acknowledging him with a quick nod. Sam had put out his hand for a shake, but when Jerome made no attempt to do the same, he withdrew it.

"Your grandmother tells me you still haven't filled out the job application."

"That's right. I've been pretty busy."

"Too busy to apply for the biggest job of your life? If they don't get applicants from inside—and let's be honest, you're the only person suited for the job at this hospital—they'll send the posting out to the public."

"Maybe that would be a good thing."

"You're talking nonsense and you know it," he scolded. The man never cared who was within hearing range when he berated her or when he was on a mission. "I'll expect to hear you've applied for the job before the end of the day."

With that, he walked away, leaving Andrea feeling humiliated and angry with him, like so many other times in her life. Did he still think she was ten? She stood and watched her father leave the cafeteria, then mumbled under her breath, "Jerk."

Sam bit his lip, watching her, probably realizing her old man treated everyone the same, including his only daughter. "You okay?"

She nodded. "Let's eat." Determined not to let on how upset she was, she led the way, taking some pleasure in the fact that Sam looked as if he wanted to deck her father.

They headed toward the line, filling their trays with the day's special soup-and-sandwich combo, tomato bisque and turkey deli. She'd been busy and hadn't realized how hungry she was, but now she'd lost her appetite, so with little thought she picked the sandwich combo. They found a table off in the corner of the cafeteria.

"You want to talk about what just happened?" Sam asked shortly after sitting.

"Absolutely not."

"Okay. Moving right along… I've been thinking about last night."

Even though she was still furious with her father, a naughty thought about their triple header last night crossed Andrea's mind and warmth trickled up her neck, spreading across her cheeks. Grateful for the respite from the tense encounter with her father, she couldn't hide her response.

"Not that, you bad girl," Sam said, lightly pinching her arm, playing along, embers igniting in those steel blue eyes.

She laughed, relieved she was back to her life as normal with the guy she was crazy about, especially those sexy eyes of his. "You don't know what I'm thinking." Yes, he did!

They shared a special smoldering gaze and smile that proved he knew exactly what she was thinking, and which set off a stream of liquid heat traveling through her navel and meandering southward. Wow, no guy had ever had such power over her that she could instantaneously forget yet another lousy meeting with her demanding father. Sam reached across the table and squeezed her hand, letting her know he felt exactly the same way. This, the sexual sparks between them, they both understood without a doubt or a single word.

She was in way over her head, with everything moving too fast, but there didn't seem to be anything she could do to stop it other than break things off. Which was the last thing she wanted to do.

He took in a slow breath and let go of her hand. They'd come to the cafeteria to eat after all. "So, anyway, what I was saying about last night refers to our conversation about your feeling like Dani's babysitter."

She'd just taken a bite of her deli turkey sandwich so she just nodded deeply and lifted her brows. Yeah, she remembered that tense conversation very well. As she recalled, she'd started it.

"I don't want you to feel like I'm using you to watch my kid, or that you are somehow considered second best in my life. Anyway, I've devised a plan to make sure you won't feel that way about this weekend."

She hadn't yet swallowed, but she did so quickly in order to ask her question. "What are you talking about?"

He took a quick spoonful of soup and continued. "I've decided to go to Mexico this weekend and I want you to come with me."

She nearly choked on what was left of her next bite of sandwich. "You're going?"

He nodded, lips tight in a straight line, the quintessential look of determination.

Just like Dad. "Just like that?"

"Cat's agreed to watch Dani so we can go with the hospital team. Medical missions are life-changing. I can't wait to share it with you."

"But, Sam, I haven't made up my mind yet." She still hadn't painted one stroke from that inspirational moment at the swings in the playground. Was he planning on taking over her life and interfering just as her father did? She tensed.

"We could have a romantic weekend away in Mexico." There went his hand again, reaching for hers and grasping her fingers.

"With the drug cartels?"

"I get it. You don't have to go if you don't want to," he said. "But I was hoping you'd go with me. I want to share it with you, have you there so you can see why I feel so committed to these trips."

"But don't you worry about Dani losing more time with you while you follow that passion for medicine and missions?"

"I know that's a touchy subject with you these days but, Andrea, as much as I love Dani, sometimes he'll have to understand that my job comes first. Not always. And certainly not because I put him second. Just that sometimes things come up that I feel called to do. This is one of them."

Why did the guy have to make such sense? "I need more time to think about this."

"You've got all afternoon and night. Those people could use your help just as much as they need mine. I can guarantee it." He shoved what was left of the half sandwich he'd been eating into his mouth and watched her.

She'd been in plenty of these positions with her father her entire life. Her back figuratively against the wall, but the words being used sounding like anything but an ultimatum. *Do this, it'll be good for you.* Part of her wanted to believe he was using one of her father's subversive techniques. But the other part, the part that knew this man was nothing like her father, nor could he ever be, understood he simply wanted to share his passion for medicine with her. This trip was special to him.

But having just come away from another tense encounter with her father, she wasn't in the proper frame of mind to give in so easily.

She sat spine straight, chin up, hands folded on her lap, not about to let him win this round, even while hating that a hospital mission to help the needy was at the center of the argument. What did that say about her? But she had to stand firm for now. "And I'd like to use all of that time to make my decision. On my terms. *If* I decide to go, it will be on *my* terms."

The man must be good at poker, because he didn't give away a single reaction to her holding out for more time. "That's perfectly understandable and reasonable." He spooned more soup into his mouth.

"Damn right it's reasonable," she mumbled. Okay, so she didn't sound quite as reasonable as he did, but maybe because she still felt as if she was talking more to her father than to Sam.

The way he lifted the corner of his mouth in a near smile proved she hadn't offended him. Did he think everything she did was cute?

When he'd finished his soup he wiped his mouth, stood, then bent to kiss her cheek. "If you make up your mind, we're leaving from the south parking lot at 6:00 a.m." He started to go but turned back. "Oh, and don't forget your passport." Then he left.

She shoved the rest of her sandwich into her mouth and chomped, irritated that Sam might be taking her for granted but also very curious about what a medical mission to Mexico would be like.

Sam was on the verge of feeling disappointed in the woman he was pretty sure he loved when he saw her beat-up champagne-colored sedan pull into the hospital parking lot at five forty-five the next morning. He'd purposely left her alone to make up her mind last night, though he'd thought about calling her any number of times. Relieved, he grinned all the way to opening the car door for her.

She tossed him a conciliatory glance as she got out. He hugged her, and she was receptive. "Glad to see you. Where's your bag?"

"In the trunk."

He found her duffel bag and several fishing-tackle boxes, but having had her make a home visit to Dani he understood that was how she carried her O&A supplies. From the backseat of the car he saw her remove a large over-the-shoulder portfolio bag. "Planning on painting?"

"Maybe. Actually, as crazy as it may sound, if time allows, it might be a way to help the kids deal with stress. We'll see."

That was exactly why he loved this lady, she was thoughtful and caring and knew how to use art for therapy. What more could he ask?

He helped her carry everything to the van he'd been assigned, making room for her belongings despite the overflowing medical supplies. With very few words but a heartfelt kiss before they left, they set out on a nearly four-hour drive across the border to Mexicali.

It had been a long and, even though it was early morning, warm drive to Baja California, then on to Mexicali and the village on the outskirts of the city of Cuernavaca. The landscape looked much like the high desert in California and long flat vistas similar to the San Fernando Valley except without all the buildings, and it struck Andrea how similar the two states were. Though poverty was more apparent here. Slowly the roads got smaller and the towns grew poorer until they were on the farthest outskirts of

Cuernavaca in a village decimated by a bomb and fire, thanks to a drug cartel.

The nearest hospital was small and overflowing, and though most of the severely injured patients had been taken there, many wounded and in need of care remained in the nearby area. Plus, as was always the case with these kinds of missions, word traveled fast and people who'd been dealing with medical issues for any number of reasons came pouring out of the countryside, looking for help.

The medical mission had been instructed to set up their makeshift clinic at the local school. They'd discussed it on the drive down and planned to divide classrooms into triage areas, patient education, easy procedures and exams, and more complex issues. A long line of people was already waiting to be seen when they arrived.

The vans were emptied of volunteers and supplies in record time and by noon the clinic was in full swing. Andrea glimpsed the dedication Sam had for helping those in need. He jumped right in and over the next several hours worked tirelessly to see and treat as many people as he could, along with the handful of other doctors, residents and nurses.

It was inspiring, and Andrea admitted she was glad she was there, even if she was nervous and felt a bit out of place. She saw her first patient with half an ear missing, made her mold of the other ear and took several pictures of what was left of the damaged side for fitting the prosthetic, then took all the information on where to mail the final product. Once again word got out and parents seemed to come crawling out of the woodwork with their kids. Some children were in need of prosthetics due to trauma and some due to a condition known as microtia. These injuries and conditions had nothing to do with the bombing, but Andrea was glad to help the community in any way she could. It turned out auricular prostheses were in high demand. Who knew?

By the end of the first day she'd seen no less than a dozen patients who needed everything from eyes to a portion of the nose and several who needed ears. She could do this, and what a joy to help little children look and feel normal again, not to mention the handful of adults who presented with missing facial parts. The only drawback was them having to wait until she went home to her workshop to make all the prosthetics and mail them back. And the prosthetic eyes wouldn't be custom-made or fitted as usual, but anything would be an improvement over an empty eye socket.

The gratitude was overwhelming, and because she didn't speak Spanish she'd smiled and nodded so much all day that by the afternoon her cheeks nearly cramped and her neck was sore.

During the evening she invited the young patients who were able to move around to come and draw pictures with her. She'd set up a little art clinic so they could dabble in just about any medium they wanted. Most stuck with pencil and drawing paper, but a few ventured into watercolors and one lone and talented teenager asked to try his hand at acrylics on canvas. She was thrilled to see them come out of their shells as they reached inside to their creative muses and worked out their fears and concerns through art. She knew firsthand the power of art and loved sharing it.

Sam caught up with her and grinned to see how engaged she'd become with the locals.

"Anyone ever tell you that you look like a canvas?"

She didn't get what he was saying until he took a rag and wiped away paint smudges from her cheeks. She laughed. "I do get messy when I'm in the zone with painting. I guess that's a good sign."

He hugged her, and after they'd shared a kiss she could see the passion for her and all things medical in his gaze, even though he looked exhausted from the long hours he'd put in. He belonged here. People in the world needed doctors like him, and a pang of guilt over her wanting him to stay home with his son made her stand straighter, and feel confused. As he'd said, sometimes Dani would have to understand that his job came first. So would she.

Life was complicated. Always would be.

"Have you got a minute?" he asked.

She looked at the group of kids deeply involved in their various projects. "Will you guys be okay without me?" She asked the one little girl who knew English to interpret for her. She repeated Andrea's question and everyone nodded and agreed they'd be fine without her for a little while. Andrea looked at the oldest boy working diligently on his small canvas. "Will you look after everyone for me?"

The little girl interpreted again, and the boy, named Rigoberto, nodded. *"Si, si."*

Sam took her hand and led her to a separate tent with a few cots inside. "Earlier I participated in surgically cleaning up a below-the-knee amputation. I want to check on Fernando."

"My God, you did major surgery here?" She glanced around at what was essentially a camping excursion setup, not a hospital.

"Actually, the bomb took care of that. The kid's leg was blown to smithereens. Good thing we brought a surgeon along. We debrided the flesh and cauterized the veins. Hopefully he didn't have too much nerve damage. For now he's stable and on pain meds and antibiotics." He went straight to a cot where a young black-haired boy slept deeply. He didn't look more than five or six.

Sam placed a gentle hand on his forehead and studied the kid, and Andrea's heart nearly broke over the compassion she saw in the man. He had so much to give, was heroic even, and didn't need to think twice about coming here once the opportunity had arisen. Unlike her. Plus he had to be an amazing doctor to do what he'd done for this young boy today.

What wasn't to like, or love, about Sam Marcus?

An IV flowed into one arm with a large fluid bag and several smaller ones, no doubt antibiotics to fight off infection in his mangled leg. In the other arm, blood was being given through the second IV. A nurse Andrea recognized from the hospital kept close vigil over the boy, who'd obviously been given something for pain.

"How's he doing, Gina?"

"Pretty good. No fever. Vitals are stable."

"Great."

A quarter of his tiny right leg was missing and heavily bandaged. "He's small for his age," Sam said to Andrea. "He's seven, and both of his parents were killed in the explosion. His uncle was the informant and they all lived together. Tomorrow we'll have to transfer him to the main hospital in Mexicali to wait for real surgery with excess bone removal and most likely skin grafts. Then after that he'll probably be put in an orphanage." He glanced up at Andrea, empathy coloring those blue eyes with concern. "Who knows what will happen to him after that."

Sam looked so sad. She understood the boy's future didn't look bright, and the ache in her chest made the backs of her eyes prick momentarily.

Sam noticed, and being the benevolent healer he was he put his arm around her. "The good news is with a below-the-knee amputation a modern prosthetic could let him walk and run almost like normal."

After one last check of the boy, Sam led her outside. "The bad news is he'll probably never get a prosthetic in an orphanage, or it will be some clunky outdated version, and he'll have to spend the rest of his life on crutches, feeling like a cripple."

"But you'll find a way to help with that, right?" If anyone could, Sam would.

He nodded, determination turning his blue eyes darker. She hugged him, thinking she loved how he couldn't walk away from children without helping in some way. He could make a difference for this one, just like the starfish parable. It was the mark of a good, good man. He had a near saint of a mother and a big family to thank for that. They stood for several moments comforting each other and Andrea considering the bad fortune in life.

Then it hit her. She didn't have the special gift Sam did, the compassion and love in his heart. She'd been left emotionally flawed because of her childhood, and it held her back in life. Her wounds weren't obvious, like Dani's or Fernando's, but they were nevertheless there. Her eyes burned and while holding Sam she let some tears flow, let him think it was because of the moving experience of the boy with the missing leg on this medical mission. Not because she felt broken inside.

Later, they slept near each other on the ground in sleeping bags, holding hands, and somehow it seemed as romantic as staying in a tropical B and B. Her world had opened up in ways she'd never dreamed of since meeting Sam. Maybe he could help heal her, too.

He'd been right about the medical mission. It had not only been life-changing, it had opened her eyes. The hard part was that she didn't like what she saw about herself.

Late Sunday afternoon they headed home. Andrea had seen how special Sam was with the sick children and finally understood without a doubt that he'd found his true calling. He was willing to make sacrifices for it, too. Though she'd been deeply moved by interacting with her share of patients, she, on the other hand, was heading home feeling a bit overwhelmed. She had a dozen or so prosthetics she'd promised to make for children and adults in the village, plus her regular work lined up at the hospital. How would she find time to do everything? Not to mention to paint that landscape she'd had on her mind since the evening at the playground.

How did Sam do it?

Why did she have to feel pulled in two directions, one practical and one artistic? Could she be a whole person if she gave up her art in order to help needy patients full-time? Wasn't there a place for art in life? Didn't it bring joy and beauty to people? She'd seen the sparkles in those kids' eyes as they'd drawn and painted, and shouldn't that be valued as much as the practical things? But she also knew she'd miss her patients. She loved helping people as much as painting.

Maybe she wasn't as emotionally deficient as she'd thought.

She forced herself to stop analyzing and worrying and once she weeded away those negative confusing feelings she realized she'd changed by coming on this mission trip. The experience had moved her deeply, she felt happy, and it had fed her creative muse in a way she hadn't experienced since college. It also made her determined to prove her father wrong. She could hold her head high and be both an ocularist and an artist, and she didn't need to run a department to prove her worth.

Now all she had to do was figure out how to make every single day longer. She'd have to get up earlier and put in time in her studio before work. She'd also have to stay late at the hospital to do the pro bono projects she'd agreed to for the people in the village. They deserved no less. She'd have to cut back on time spent with Sam and Dani, which pained her, but if she wanted to do it all, and she really did, there had to be sacrifices. A sick feeling dashed around her stomach and circled her heart. Sam would understand, but would Dani?

"How're you feeling?" Sam asked, taking her hand in his.

"Exhausted. Elated. Overwhelmed." She glanced at him through newly wise eyes and he still looked gorgeous. "Surprisingly, pretty good."

"Are you glad you came?"

"You know I am. Seeing you with the children, especially with Fernando, made me realize what a gift you have. It made me realize how lucky Dani is to have you as his father. But it also made me face myself. Your childhood turned you into the person you are and so did mine. But, unlike you, I don't think I'll ever have what it takes to be a parent."

"What are you talking about? You're great with Dani."

"Because I'm not his parent. I'm not responsible for him. You are."

Sam gave her a skeptical glance. "Something tells me there's more going on than meets the eye here. Are you okay?"

"To be honest, no. I'm not okay. This weekend I realized how messed up I am. You can open your heart and reach out to help people when I want to run scared. Loving others means something totally different to you than it does to me. My mother loves my father and it has nearly destroyed her."

"You talk as though your father is a monster."

"Not obviously so, but you saw how he was with me in the cafeteria. He still talks to me like I'm ten. He has zero respect for me or my mother. He was the kind of dad who'd demand I get straight As in school, then not bother to show up at the awards assembly. I'd be the only kid there without a parent in the room, because my mother was too timid to ever learn how to drive."

Andrea hated sounding so lost and needy, but she and Sam had been raised completely differently. He had the confidence to do whatever he felt he should, completely independent, interestingly enough, not needing anyone. Or anyone's approval. Sam needed to know why she was mistrusting and hesitant.

"My dad would holler and carry on if things weren't perfect at home, then rarely ever be there. I never felt love from him. All I ever felt was lonely and miserable, and I'm afraid I don't know how to feel or show love because of him."

Sam drew her near and snuggled her close. "You're not anything like your father. Don't try to fool yourself."

Bitter thoughts and intense sadness made her eyes prickle. Sam believed in her. He saw something worthwhile in her. He wanted to encourage her to branch out and experience a different kind of life. A different kind of love?

He put his arm around her on the van bench and pulled her near. "This probably isn't the ideal time to say it, but I thought you should know—" he kissed her cheek "—that I love you."

CHAPTER EIGHT

SAM HELD ANDREA close in the hospital parking lot. He cupped her face and kissed her as if they hadn't seen each other in weeks, even though they'd just spent two full days together. She let him kiss her, not caring what anyone thought. The man had already taken her breath away when he'd told her he loved her a few short moments ago, and she wanted to make sure he knew how happy that'd made her.

Especially after she'd just confessed how messed up her family was, and how it had affected her, and the man had still said it. She kissed him hard. Everyone was busy unloading the vans; they'd probably never even notice what she and Sam were up to.

Was she really worth loving? In Sam's world, yes. He had the capacity to love as she'd never experienced.

She wrapped her arms around his neck and leaned into his kiss with everything she had, and had never felt more beautiful in her life. Except for the fact they were both fairly grungy after a weekend of hard work without a shower, and her short hair, except for a few spikes, was nearly matted flat to her head. Yet she still felt beautiful... because Sam had said he loved her.

They'd made it back to St. Francis of the Valley Hospital parking lot by 8:00 p.m. There was much to be done, but his lips and the cascade of thrills they caused were the center of her world at the moment. She'd never been kissed by a man who loved her before. Wow, even her toes inside her practical cross-trainers curled from this most special of all kisses.

"Can we get a hand here, lovebirds?" said Anthony, the shaggy-haired, bearded resident who'd initiated the medical mission, standing over by one of the vans.

Nearly dizzy from the kiss, Andrea parted her lips from Sam's and looked into his eyes. She'd never seen such a dreamy gaze from him before and she savored the moment. Could she really do that to him? Well, it was a big deal when a guy told a woman he loved her. It had to be the honest-to-God truth or it meant nothing. Everything seemed surreal and it took a couple of seconds to check back in with the real world. She crawled out from the lingering love-hazed moment with him, not wanting it to end but knowing she needed to help with the unpacking.

"Welcome home," Sam said, sending a million possibilities through her brain for a meaning to that phrase.

"Thank you for inviting me," she said, heartfelt. The weekend had been inspiring on a dozen levels. Now that she realized how emotionally mixed up she was, she could work on fixing it. She could change if she tried. Sam would help her.

Sam tossed a look over his shoulder. "Theoretically, Anthony's the one who invited you."

"Yeah," Anthony broke in, "and I'm the one who needs your help unpacking now. Please, guys?"

Grinning, they got busy chipping in with the business of emptying and cleaning out the vans. Before long, when everything had been completed, Sam was at her side again.

"I've got to take off to pick up Dani. I promised him he'd sleep in his own bed tonight."

"I understand. Give him a hug for me."

"You're not coming over?" Surprise tented his eyebrows.

"We've just spent nearly forty-eight hours together. I love you, Sam Marcus, but right now I really need a shower and a good night's sleep."

She'd driven her own car over and had—despite the novelty of having a man tell her he loved her and her believing him—decided to go home tonight, leaving Dani and Sam time together. They needed father-son time, having been parted the whole weekend. Besides, she needed to get serious about a new routine, painting early in the morning before going to work. That special picture was fighting to get put on canvas.

He kissed her again, more a peck of understanding than a real kiss. "Okay. I'll see you in the morning, then."

"Lunch?"

"You're on."

She stood for a few moments, watching the man she loved walk away, wondering over the sudden change in her relationship status. She looked down at her feet to make sure they were still touching the ground. Maybe happiness was finally within her reach. The thought started a whole new tumble of chills.

Then she saw the text from her father.

We need to talk. ASAP. Come for dinner tomorrow night.

It wasn't an invitation so much as a summons.

The thought about falling in love and walking on air dissolved. Look what falling in love and marrying the man of her dreams had done for her mother. She'd often tried to make up for their being alone by telling Andrea about the wonderfully amazing man he'd been when they'd dated. Her mother's love for her father had turned out to be a deeply destructive emotion that had escorted her mother into a dark chamber, left her alone, moody and often withdrawn. Love had eaten her alive.

If she wasn't careful, could the same happen to her?

Andrea asked Sam and Dani to accompany her to her parents' house on Monday night as backup, but not before checking with her mother to see if it would be okay. Plus she needed to feel Mom out, see how her new meds were working. Was her depression under control? Was she really up for a dinner party, no matter how casual? They'd had a great time a couple of weeks ago, eating, talking, but that had been just the two of them. Adding Dad into the mix was always a gamble.

Barbara had promised she was in good spirits and would love to meet Sam and Dani, so Andrea had invited them along. It wasn't fair to use Sam as a buffer, but Andrea had something on her mind she wanted to be firm about, and having Sam there would give her more confidence.

Rather than knock on the door at the huge Rimmer family home in the heart of the Los Feliz hills above Los Angeles, she used her old house key and let them all in.

"Hello? We're here! Mom?"

"Come on in," Mom said, appearing at the kitchen door, wiping her hands on her half apron.

Andrea rushed to her mother and gave her a hug, grateful she had a spark of life in her brown eyes today. "Mom, this is Sam and Dani."

Perhaps overreacting a tad, Barbara put her hands on her cheeks and beamed. "It's so wonderful to meet you," she said to Sam, taking his hand and shaking it enthusiastically. Then she bent forward to greet Dani. "Well, hello, young man. Aren't you a handsome boy."

Dani blushed and hid behind Sam's leg. "Sorry, he's a bit shy," Sam stepped in.

"We'll have plenty of time to get to know each other, won't we, young man?"

Still hiding, Dani peeked around Sam's leg to take another look at the new woman.

Barbara's voice actually sounded cheery, but Andrea didn't trust it. She'd had too much experience with her mother's mood swings over the years. She tensed, hoping for the best, but part of her was waiting cautiously.

Her mother twisted her wedding ring round and round her finger, a sign that underneath the cheery exterior she was nervous. "Why don't we go into the other room."

The Rimmer house was a grand old 1920s-style home with every room fairly small and neatly partitioned off, with a tendency toward being dark and dreary because of it. A perfect setting for her depressed mother. Andrea had forgotten how claustrophobic the house could feel at times. They walked through the living room section, with furniture that probably hadn't been sat on for months, and into the wood-paneled den that connected to the dining room.

"Can we help with anything, Mom?"

"You can get everyone drinks and set the table if you'd like."

Andrea and Sam pitched in and got everything ready at the table, letting Dani have a glass of lemonade while they did so.

In the dining room, Sam reached for Andrea's arm and squeezed it. "Everything will be okay." She'd filled Sam in on her mother's condition on the ride over, and he already knew firsthand the blustery personality of her father. "I'm here for you."

"Thanks." She believed him and it reassured her.

The front door opened and a cool draft entered the house, traveling all the way to the den. Her father was home, and the loose knot that had been forming in her stomach over the family dinner tightened.

"Good evening," Jerome said, making his appearance wearing a dark blue work suit and still acting all business.

Dani went back into hiding behind Sam's leg. Barbara appeared from the kitchen, still twisting the ring on her finger but this time even faster, a new anxious expression on her face. Jerome went to her and kissed her cheek. "Barbara, something smells good."

Poof, tension disappeared from her eyes, and the ring-twisting stopped. "It's your favorite, Jerry, Santa Barbara–styled tri tip with onions and bell peppers."

Turning his attention to Andrea, Jerome ignored Barbara's reply. "I have a bone to pick with you, young lady." He said it as if she'd been truant from school.

Andrea squared her shoulders. "If it's about the job application for department administrator, I'm going to be honest. I don't want the job."

"You don't want the job? Do you know how many people would die for that job? The benefits, the stability, the future?"

"I like the job I have."

His jaw clamped down and his eyes went steely. Rather than wither, as she might have as a child, Andrea stood her ground.

"Do you honestly think I got you that apprenticeship so you could settle for working part-time?"

"Frankly, Father, I don't care why you forced me to take the apprenticeship. I've done what you wanted, will get my credential within the year, and after that I can do anything I want with it."

If steam could come out of a person's ears, it would have right then and there from Jerome.

"Why don't we all take a break from this conversation and have dinner," Barbara spoke up, sounding firmer than

Andrea expected, which surprised and pleased her. Since when had Mom become a mediator? Out of respect for her mother, and little Dani, she'd bite back all the words she'd truly love to sling at her father right then.

As everyone prepared to sit at the dining table, Jerome cast a sideways glance at Andrea. "We're not through with this conversation."

Andrea pressed her lips together and passed her father an oh-yes-we-are stare, just long enough to get her point across.

The new medications for depression seemed to be doing wonders for Barbara. She sat at the dining table, head held high, making light conversation with Sam and teasing Dani to coax him to eat. Surprisingly, even Jerome settled in to a more welcoming mood as the family and guests enjoyed the grilled beef, fingerling potatoes and a vegetable medley casserole. Maybe he'd finally understood that his daughter could be as strong-willed as he was.

With Sam at her side, ready to back her up, Andrea had found confidence enough to make her point. It was her life. She'd make all the decisions from here on. Thank you very much, *Daddy*.

Things were going great for the next couple of weeks. Andrea kept to her schedule of painting every morning before work and only spending the weekends with Sam and Dani. They might say they loved each other, but she still longed for independence, and he needed special father-son time. Plus not going over to his house during the week made Sam all the happier to see her when she spent Friday nights through Sunday evenings with him and Dani. Even then, Sam respected her need to paint in the mornings. And after the boy went to bed they definitely made up for those lost nights together.

With this schedule, the picture that had been impatiently waiting inside her head seemed to pour out onto the canvas, as if it had commandeered the brushes and all she had to do was let her arms do the grunt work. She hadn't been this inspired in ages, and whether it was from being in a solid relationship with a good man whom she loved or from going to Mexico and helping out people in need, she figured her life had definitely taken a turn for the better.

Soon that painting would be done, and she'd already finished a couple of the prosthetics she'd promised to the children in Mexico, too. And, as if her positive message was circulating in the universe, a long-ago friend from art school had contacted her about a few of her earlier paintings. A new café wanted to display art on their walls in the Gas Light District of San Diego. It would be a huge help in getting her noticed, and Andrea was so excited she wanted to personally deliver the paintings and spend a weekend catching up with her old friend. Sam understood and completely supported her going.

It seemed amazing what a woman could accomplish when she was in love.

Even more amazing, Sam had found a second babysitter. The teenager of one of his colleagues from the hospital needed extra money for a big school trip in the fall. Ally was more than willing to babysit on weeknights if or whenever Sam needed her, and, most important, Dani liked her. Yes, all seemed right with the world.

On the eve of her trip to San Diego, a full two weeks from the night she'd lost sleep making her decision to take Sam and the young resident up on their offer to go along on the medical mission, she found herself in a very different situation. She was definitely losing sleep, but this time for a far more exciting reason.

Sam held her hips as she straddled him and rocked his world, doing a fantastic job of rocking her world, too. Quite sure there was no way her breasts could get any tighter or more tingly, he surprised her by rising up on an elbow and taking one into his mouth. She stopped briefly to savor the thrumming throughout her body, but soon craving more she lifted and curved over his length, with him solid and bucking up into her. The benefits of being on top and positioning him just so fanned the heat building between her thighs to a near inferno.

With early signs that there'd be no turning back, tension coiled behind her navel, knotting and threading down, spiraling deeper into her core. The small of her back buzzed with sensations. Every cell seemed awake and vibrating thanks to him. Sam's mouth soon found her other breast as she leaned over him, and he held her hips in place when he drove up into her again and again. Nearly helpless against his thrusts, all she could do was hold steady, willing her arms not to give out.

Rhythmical currents rushed along every nerve ending as he came at her over and over, licking at her mounting fuse, pushing and prodding harder, then faster, sustaining the thrill, and suspending time in that sublime state. He kept on until he set off a deep implosion in her. A guttural sound escaped her mouth, she trembled over him, the sweeping sensations annihilating every thought as her body tumbled and rolled through bliss.

Relentless, he carried on, pulling every last shudder and quiver out of her. Then, reading her perfectly, knowing she was basking in the afterglow, he rolled her onto her back. Determined and lost inside her, on his knees he came at her from the top, hitching her legs over his shoulders, grasping her pelvis tightly over him, holding her in place, bearing down on her. Deeper and faster still he came at her; hard and unyielding, he reawakened her center, then drove her passion so she soon needed him again like breath itself. His undivided attention lifted her, making her soar with inward spiraling sensations, then quickly dropping her into freefall in the nick of time to join him in his earth-shaking climax.

They crumpled together in a heap on the sheets, panting, their skin glowing with moisture as if they'd just run a two-hundred-meter dash. They clung to each other, Andrea never more grateful for knowing a man in her life. He laid a wet and wild final kiss on her and they moaned in mutual satisfaction. Damn, he was good.

She curled into him and they cuddled for several ecstatic minutes in the dark, their sweet love scenting the room. His fingers lightly dancing over her arm and backside, he drew her nearer and placed a kiss on her neck.

As she slowly emerged from her sexual stupor, something niggled at the back of her mind. Sam had seemed preoccupied throughout dinner. Was he worried about her going away? More than once she'd wanted to ask if something was bothering him, but in all honesty was afraid to find out it might be her. Or them. Or the new relationship they were forging.

The only example of love she'd had growing up had been her domineering father and her deeply depressed mother. It had definitely affected her ability to trust in love. But Sam had proved he was completely different from her father, and she was no longer afraid to hold back, to let herself trust and love him with everything she had. She was on the verge of feeling she'd found the right man, that she finally belonged somewhere, with him, and didn't want to upset her cart of dreams.

So she kept her concerns to herself about his earlier quiet demeanor. When he'd made it known that he wanted her after putting Dani to bed, she gave herself to him completely. It had quickly become second nature, almost like an addiction. Now, languishing in his embrace, she didn't want to be anywhere else.

He cleared his throat. Her ears perked up.

"I've been doing a lot of thinking," he said, his arm tightening around her as he spoke.

She hadn't been wrong about something being on his mind. She barely breathed for fear of missing what he was about to say. "Yes?"

"I've been thinking about Fernando in Mexico."

The weight of the universe seemed to come crashing down on her. Stunned, she couldn't take a complete breath. As thoroughly relaxed as she'd been a single moment before, she was now a ball of tension. "You're not saying you want to adopt him, too, are you?"

"I'm seriously thinking about it, and I want to know your opinion."

She sat up, because in her confusion she couldn't bring herself to lie beside him right now, and she needed to see his face. "You want my opinion?"

His lower lip rolled tightly inward; he bit it. "I'm saying I can't get Fernando out of my mind. I swear the ghost of my mother is prodding me to get that boy, somehow, someway."

How could she be honest about her feelings and not come off as selfish when at the core was a noble desire? Sam's compassion seemed to be endless. Regardless, she owed it to him to tell him her thoughts. "You're setting this up to make me look and feel like a horrible person if I don't clap my hands and say 'Gee, that's great. Do it. Right now.' But if we're going to be a couple, you owe it to me to consult me on this kind of thing." Wasn't the decision to adopt a kid monumentally important?

He rubbed his hand along her shoulder and arm in an appeasing manner, and it irritated her. "Which is exactly what I'm doing."

She shook her head, refusing to make eye contact, reverting right back to not trusting him, to thinking he was just like her father. Old habits died hard.

"Life doesn't give us courtesy pauses, Andrea. You saw him. That kid needs a shot at a decent life."

Did this go beyond compassion to a savior complex? "Do you plan to save the whole world? Because the supply of kids who deserve chances is endless."

She may have hit hard and careless, but she stood by her comments. Stoic, he stared at the bedspread. Had he honestly thought she'd be overjoyed?

"You're a doctor, you help children stay healthy, isn't that enough?" He probably hated her right now, thinking she was callous and self-centered. Unworthy of his love.

She should have known the kind of person he was the instant she'd seen the Legend of the Starfish framed and hanging on his family room wall. In perfect calligraphy on parchment paper, the moral of the story came through loud and clear, that though one person can't save every single starfish stranded on the beach... *I can make a difference to that one, and that one, and...*

"I just can't get Fernando out of my head."

He was a true believer in the philosophy, thanks to his mother, a good, almost mythical woman she would never be able to measure up to. Who'd quite possibly died young from working herself to the bone with so many kids.

She hated letting her emotions take over, but feeling defeated before they'd ever even gotten started her eyes prickled and watered. No sooner had she fallen in love, finally giving herself permission for the new and amazing feeling, she'd had it ripped away by a guy who couldn't live with himself unless he adopted children in need.

"Aren't there ways to help him without adopting him? You could arrange for one of those high-tech prosthetic legs for him. Donate money to the orphanage where he'll live."

"You're right, but I'm just saying I can't get him out of my mind. It hurts."

There had to be more to the pain he mentioned than Sam's need to rescue kids. "Where does it come from?" His eyes darted away from hers but she couldn't let him drop the subject, especially with her going away in the morning. "This compulsion of yours, where does it come from?"

He looked back at her and his eyes, thanks to the dim moonlight, looked opaque and pleaded with her. "I haven't been completely honest with you."

A foreboding brick-like weight settled on her chest. Oh, God, he hadn't already planned to adopt the kid and lied when he'd said he wanted her opinion, had he?

He reached for her hand and squeezed it. "There's something I haven't told you."

In fear, but needing to know the truth above all else, she held his hand with both of hers and engaged his eyes. "Tell me, Sam. What?" He didn't respond immediately, as if it was the hardest thing in the world to tell her, so her wild imagination took root. He really had already made plans to adopt this boy. The impact on their new relationship would be more than she could take. Hadn't he learned anything with Katie? "Look, I'm not your mother. I'm sorry for not being a saint. I'm just getting used to Dani, and to be honest so are you. It's too soon for me. I'm not even sure if I could be a decent parent to Dani. Don't you see?"

One eyebrow crimped upward. His look of disappointment may as well have been a dagger to her chest. The fairy tale of love with a wonderful guy evaporated into thin air. Hadn't she learned her lesson from her mother about how destructive love could be? Did he love her for herself, or did he just see her as someone he could mold into a version of his bighearted mother? Maybe he was like her father after all, wanting to change her and dictate her life. Would she only be a way for Sam to have that big family he planned to get by any means necessary? Her brain whirled with questions. None of them good. The thought of him giving her an ultimatum made her feel queasy. The words *the end* came to mind.

"That's not it. I promise I haven't gone behind your back and already made plans for Fernando." He squeezed her fingers, and she felt relieved. "I haven't been honest about my family."

Her mind went suddenly still, waiting, worrying, not having a clue what he was about to say. Sam had always come on like a steamroller, wanting that big family just like the one he'd grown up in, on his timeline and terms. Andrea had stood her ground, being honest no matter how unappealing that may have come across to Sam. One adopted son per single father was more than enough. But there was something about his family he needed to come clean about, and she suspected adoption had nothing to do with it.

"I've let you think I'd come from one big happy family, and in a way I did. But it wasn't my family."

She canted her head, holding her breath over what he might say next.

"That picture out there…" He gestured to his living room. "It's my foster family. *I* was the kid who got taken in by them. The Murphys." A blank stare overtook his face, as if a deeply sad memory fought to take control. "I was ten. I was taken away from my mother for being left alone at night. She was young and single and had to work two jobs to keep us from being homeless. It had been going on off and on since I was eight. She'd been warned on a couple of occasions, and finally one of the neighbors called the authorities. The Murphy family took me in and when my mother never tried to get me back, they kept me until I was eighteen. I've pretended to be something I'm not. I'm sorry. Truth is I'm an only child, just like you."

Love, sadness, anger, compassion and a dozen other

emotions swirled around Andrea. How must a young child feel, being left alone night after night? Talk about feeling abandoned. No wonder he wanted to rescue kids. The hair on her arms stood on end over his revelation. She wrapped her arms around him, holding him tight, loving him more than she could bear to feel. "I'm so sorry, and so grateful to that family." She looked at him. He seemed to be in shock at reliving the toughest moments of his life.

"I wanted to be a part of a family more than anything, and they let me. When I was eighteen, my foster mom helped me look for my birth mother. She'd gotten married, started a new family, and when she could have tried to get me back, she hadn't." His face contorted on the last phrase, but only for an instant before he wrestled back control.

Andrea held him tighter, her heart aching for him.

"My own mother didn't want me, but Mom Murphy did. They accepted me as part of the family, and Cat, too. She was one of the other foster kids. Foster kids came and went, but the Murphys kept Cat and me. We bonded like sister and brother, right along with the other Murphy kids. I was lucky. I guess you could say blessed."

"Oh, Sam." She didn't know what to say. All she knew was that he was a special man. He'd received the grace of a strong woman after being left behind by his struggling mother. He'd had a second chance, like those starfish. No wonder that story meant so much to him. His foster mom had made a difference in his life, but Andrea suspected that even that wasn't enough to erase the pain of having his mother let him go and never try to get him back, even when she could have.

Andrea kissed the man she loved, in that moment knowing he could never be anything like her father. He knew what it was like to feel completely alone, to be frightened, to be saved. Because of that, she suspected she had a lot of making up to do for the women in his life who'd walked away from him, starting with his mother and ending with Katie. At some deep level would Sam always mistrust *her*? Would she have to prove herself over and over to him?

They held each other for several long moments, soothing, reassuring, loving, then found themselves back in bed, *showing* exactly how much they cared.

Late Sunday afternoon Sam jumped to answer the phone when he saw Andrea's number on the screen. He'd given her space by not calling her all weekend. Hell, after what he'd laid on her he was afraid to find out what she thought, because he loved her so much. He'd figured that out for sure over the past two days.

"Hi!" she said breathlessly. "I'm just walking into the house. You won't believe what happened in San Diego."

Wanting more than anything to see her, to hold her in his arms, he jumped in. "Why don't you come over for dinner and tell me all about it."

An hour later, she rushed through his door and into his arms, her excitement obvious.

He kissed her and she eagerly kissed him back. "I sold a painting yesterday! And another couple commissioned me to paint a modern art version of their cat!" She laughed. "It's absurd, I know, but I've already got an idea for it."

"That's fantastic," he said, meaning it. He was thrilled for her.

"For the first time since art school I see the possibility of making some decent money, painting and selling my art without selling out, you know?"

"Sounds like it's a good start." He measured his tone, not wanting to sound like the voice of caution, but part of him worried she'd take this bit of success and blow it out of proportion.

"I know! I'm ecstatic." Her eyes glimmered and her

cheeks were flushed, and seeing her so animated and having missed her so deeply after she'd left early on Saturday morning, the only thing he wanted to do was kiss her again.

Of course he wanted to help her in any way possible to achieve success, had probably already overstepped his bounds by talking to hospital administration about her paintings. Coming from her background, with a manipulative and overbearing father, she needed to prove to herself she was in control.

Man, she's going to hit the roof if she finds out I put in a good word for her at St. Francis's.

They kissed more. He let his concerns go and focused back on showing how happy he was to see her. If Dani hadn't wandered out from his room and tugged on both of their jeans, they probably would have wound up having sex on the couch.

Oh, wait, right, since he'd become a father, those days were over…until later after he put Dani to bed, anyway.

Monday morning, after spending the night at Sam's, having incredible I-missed-you-for-one-whole-day-and-a-half sex, Andrea still managed to get up extra early with her alarm. She headed home, took a quick shower and put in an hour painting her favorite project. The enormous canvas as seen through a modern art lens, complete with a kid on a swing and a long-legged faceless dad pushing him, was really shaping up. The fact that the boy held a starfish in his hand was a new, surprising addition and tickled her.

She arrived at work to see a construction crew tearing down part of the hospital lobby. Was it an omen? She remembered getting the memo about the remodeling project scheduled for this month, but had thought nothing about it until right now. Remodeling meant redecorating. Those tired old print excuses for art on the faded walls needed to come down and never be seen again. She had a damn good suggestion for their replacements, too.

As she headed toward the elevator she wondered who she needed to talk to about her own paintings. The display in the trendy café in San Diego had been a huge hit. Maybe the hospital might consider doing something similar here? Showcase local starving artists? Heck, she knew several artists in the area who'd give their eyeteeth to show their work in a busy place like the lobby of St. Francis of the Valley, including her!

She opened the O&A department with her mind spinning over the possibilities, then saw an envelope from Administration that had been slipped under the door. Once she read the contents, she rushed to call the one person she wanted to share every part of her life with—Sam.

"You won't believe this!" She didn't give Sam a chance to say hello, but he had a sneaky suspicion what she was referring to, since he'd started the ball rolling. "The hospital wants to discuss my art. They've gone to my website and seen my work, they're especially interested in my eye and keyhole painting, and they're interested in seeing more samples of my work in person! I've got an appointment with them on Wednesday. The note says, if they get approval, they'd put my pictures in the lobby entrance."

Since Andrea had finally stopped to take a breath, Sam jumped in while he could. "That's fantastic!" A twinge of guilt and a pang of anxiety gnawed at his conscience. Had he screwed up? What if she asked who had given them her name? Should he tell her first?

"I know! Nothing is definite but, wow, maybe with a few more sales and opportunities like this, I can actually support myself painting!"

What? Why should she immediately start talking about walking away from everything she'd worked toward over the past four years of her apprenticeship? That possibility had never occurred to him because of the great relationships she had with her patients. Shaken, he wasn't sure what to say. It seemed his great idea might have backfired on multiple levels.

"I mean, I may be getting ahead of myself but, really, Sam, do you see what I'm talking about?"

"I do. The hospital lobby display would be a huge opportunity."

"Oh, man, I never thought I'd see the day."

Still shaken, he wanted to ask, *Has it been that bad? Is it so terrible to use your gifts to help people replace missing ears and eyes?* Would he come off as a wet rag over her flame if he brought that up now? Or, worse yet, would he seem totally selfish and overbearing, just like her father, expecting her to stay in a job that she, apparently, could walk away from at the drop of a hat?

Perhaps his biggest offense—now that he understood how important it was for Andrea to step out from under her father's overreaching grasp—had been going behind the scenes and manipulating the outcome. Would she be furious with him for making that appointment for her in the first place if she found out?

Ah, so much for his big ideas.

CHAPTER NINE

SAM EXAMINED THE five-year-old Hispanic girl. His first observation made him think of Andrea. The child had been born with microtia, a condition where the pinna or auricle was underdeveloped. In this case, the right outer ear was extremely undersized compared to the normal left one. He hadn't seen this condition for a few years, even though the statistical incidence was one in six to twelve thousand births.

According to the chart, not only was the patient new to him, it was the first visit on record at St. Francis of the Valley. A small notation at the bottom referred to the family being new immigrants and first-time medically insured in the United States.

"The good news," he said, wanting to help the young mother's concerned expression, "is that the ear canal seems perfectly normal. I'll order a hearing test to make sure of that. Okay?"

The mother nodded eagerly.

"More good news," he continued. "There is surgery for this if you are interested."

Again, her eyes grew wide with interest.

"But Letitia needs to grow a little more first." He emphasized the fact by tickling the child, making her giggle. "You need to eat your vegetables, kiddo." The child laughed more. He turned to the mother. "You may want to think long and hard about the surgery. It involves using rib cartilage to make a graft and the surgery goes in stages, so there will be three different procedures over a period of time. We recommend the surgery the summer before Letitia begins school, and we have an excellent pediatric surgeon on staff who specializes in this."

"Three surgeries?" Worry lining her forehead like a pyramid, she shook her head.

"Another option is to have an ear prosthetic made. We have one of the best departments in the country right here. They can match your daughter's other ear with a silicone lookalike."

"She doesn't have to wait? No surgery?"

"There is need for one small procedure to create a way to attach the prosthetic ear, unless you want to use adhesive tape every day."

"One procedure?"

He nodded. "But Letitia would have to take the ear off every night. If she got sunburned, her ear wouldn't. That sort of thing. But I can guarantee that with our expert anaplastologists you'll have to look extra close to tell the difference from her natural ear."

"I have much to think about," Letitia's mother said.

"Yes. And I haven't even begun the actual physical. Let's get started, okay?"

Armed with options, the child's mother appeared more confident as Sam began the otherwise well-child routine physical examination of Letitia.

He understood that sometimes little kids made fun of anyone who didn't look like them. He'd thought long and hard about it regarding Dani. And as Letitia might start kindergarten soon, her mother would be worried about her, though the child's long thick hair did a good job of covering much of the tiny, underdeveloped ear.

He also suspected, from the mother's acne scars, that she may have been on a medication in early pregnancy that was known to cause the condition. The last thing he wanted to do was to make the mother feel responsible for a condition that really couldn't be pinpointed to any one thing she may or may not have done during pregnancy. So he kept his thoughts to himself. His job was to give a physical and maybe help the child look and feel more like the other kids in school, and that he could definitely do.

Andrea had been on his mind nonstop since her trip to San Diego, and especially since she'd hinted about trying to make a go of her artistic career. Did it mean she'd want to give up the one here at the hospital? Wasn't helping people, and especially children like little Letitia here, to feel good about themselves a noble job, too? Of course he'd support her in any decision she made because he loved her and wanted her to be happy, but he knew she had so much to offer St. Francis Hospital.

"Dr. Marcus." Sam's nurse tapped on the examination room door. "Dr. Begozian needs to talk to you."

Sam had just finished the PE. "Can you give Mrs. Juarez the instructions to the lab and Audiology?"

The nurse nodded, so he said goodbye and slipped out of the room to take the call. "Let me know what you decide," he said when he reached the door.

"I will, Doctor."

Sam headed to his office and the phone with the blinking light.

"I need a huge favor, Sam," said Greg Begozian, a young and bright resident whom Sam had taken under his wing.

"What's up?"

"I'm supposed to work the ER tonight, but I just got word my father's had a heart attack, and I need to catch a plane to Sacramento ASAP. But all the other residents are tied up."

"I'm sorry to hear about your father. Is he stable?"

"For now. Looks like he needs a bypass graft. I don't have the full story just yet."

"Hey, don't worry about tonight. I've got you covered."

"Thanks, Sam. You never let me down."

Sam hung up, thinking he'd be letting Dani down tonight, though, by having someone else read him his bedtime story and tucking him in. Ever since Andrea had brought up the touchy topic he'd thought a lot about it. But he was a doctor, and he felt responsible for his residents. At least he had an extra babysitter these days, one who would come to his house so Dani could go to sleep in his own bed. And Andrea didn't necessarily need to even know about tonight, did she?

Unfortunately, as it turned out an hour later, Andrea would need to know about tonight, because Ally wasn't available and Cat had other plans, so he needed to ask her to watch Dani. He hated making the call because he knew how seriously she was taking her painting now. Plus she had the appointment scheduled with hospital admin on Wednesday.

Fifteen minutes later...

"Uh, Andrea, I hate to interfere with any plans you have for tonight, but Ally has a volleyball playoff game and Cat has parent-teacher conferences, and one of my residents has a family emergency, so I'll need to cover for him."

"And?" Ever since seeing Sam in action in Mexico, she understood the demands of Sam's job and the pressure he was under, but before then she'd really given him a hard time about not being around enough for Dani. She understood the hesitation in his voice right now, but the guy had a serious problem with admitting he needed her.

"And I need someone to watch Dani."

"Was that so hard to ask?"

"I know you've got a lot of projects in the works now…"

"I'll bring my sketch pad and work after I put Dani to bed." Determination to make both her relationship with Sam and her personal achievements work was her new goal.

"You'll do it?"

Did he need to sound so surprised? "Yes. Since I'm your last resort, I'll do it."

"It's time to sleep, my love, my love…" Andrea whisper-read to Dani from an especially pretty book, as he settled comfortably into the crook of her arm. She'd personally chosen the children's book because of the beautiful pictures painted by the author. Each page seemed worth framing. But only after reading the truck book with all the bright pictures and hands-on activities. Reading this one, the time-to-sleep book, was her favorite way to calm the boy down.

Dani yawned wide and long after she'd read only a few pages of dreamy places with unusual animals and sleeping children. He rubbed his eyes.

"Are you ready for bed, sweetie?"

He nodded. She'd helped him brush his teeth already, and they'd had a fun game of hide-and-seek before that. To be honest, she loved being with Dani and when she was with him and Sam, her painting rarely entered her mind. That worried her. Wasn't art supposed to be first and foremost to a serious artist?

She walked him to his bed and helped him in, then tucked the sheets around him. "How's that?"

He nodded, smiling. "I like you to put me to bed." His speech had grown by leaps and bounds, too.

"I like putting you to bed." She kissed his forehead,

savoring the preciousness of the little person and his fresh bath smell.

"I wish you lived with us."

She'd started to reach to turn out the lamp but stopped midway. How was she supposed to respond to that? Even wondered if Sam might have put his kid up to it. That made her smile, knowing how absurd the thought was. She decided to take the change-the-subject route. "You're a lucky boy to have your daddy."

"He works."

Too much. She didn't need to finish the sentence for Dani; she knew exactly what he'd meant. "Because he loves you and wants to take good care of you."

"I like you to put me to bed."

"That makes me happy, Dani. Thank you." *And sad for Sam. Oh, man, things are getting more complicated and downright awkward.*

"Will you hug me?" he asked in his usual shy manner.

How could she not hug this sweet, sweet boy? She wrapped her arms around Dani and held him until he gave a signal that he was ready to let go. "Sweet dreams, my little man."

Just as she got to the door he whispered, "I love you."

No doubt he'd heard it hundreds of times from his dad. What could she say? "I love you, too." It was true. She loved Dani with everything she had. She'd fallen hard for him the first night she'd met him. Now both of the Marcus men had declared their love for her. She gazed at Dani snuggled into his pillow, looking so small in his twin bed.

The poor kid had lost his parents before he could remember them, but he instinctively knew he wanted a family. Sam had been a blessing to the boy, just as the Murphys had been a blessing to him, and Andrea felt honored to be a part of his life. But Dani obviously wanted them together, like a real family. Which put both Sam and Andrea in a tough position.

After Dani had gone to sleep Andrea sketched some preliminary drawings, using the photograph of the cat from the couple who'd commissioned her to paint it. It was hard to concentrate, knowing that she had to tell Sam what she'd discovered tonight, but soon enough she got lost in drawing. It was almost eleven when he got home.

His eyes looked weary and his posture imperceptibly stooped, but enough for her to notice. Whenever she saw him her heart felt full, and that had never happened with anyone else. She walked toward him, and they hugged. He felt so good to hold.

"How'd things go?" he asked after she kissed him hello.

"Good. Dani's the sweetest kid I've ever met. But you already know that." She didn't mean to let emotion take over, but her voice had caught on *ever* and now there was stinging behind her eyelids.

It didn't get past Sam. "You okay?"

"Yeah. Can I make you a sandwich or anything?" She tried to recover fast, but moisture gathered at the sides of her eyes.

"To hell with the sandwich." His posture straightened, concern tinting his eyes. "Did something happen here tonight?" He came closer, looked into her face.

She swallowed against a sudden thickening in her throat. *Dani told me he loved me.* "Your son misses you so much, Sam."

A snap of emotion changed the concern in his eyes to irritation. She'd obviously hit a sensitive spot. "Look, a resident's father had a heart attack. He couldn't find anyone to replace him, so I agreed to work tonight."

"I get it. I know you have a demanding job. I'm just saying he misses you." *And now he's foolishly decided to love me, and I'm not ready for that responsibility.*

"And sometimes he'll have to understand that working late comes with the territory."

"But he's so young." She couldn't allow herself to get sidetracked. Dani's sad little-boy confession that his father worked a lot had set off bad memories. "Do you have any idea what it was like, never seeing my dad? Wondering if he cared?"

"You think you're the only one who ever wondered that? It's a fact of life. Being a foster kid with loads of brothers and sisters ensures you never get as much attention as a kid wants." He went quiet, turning inward.

How quickly she'd forgotten how frightening the first ten years of his life must have been. She needed to hear and understand his side of the story. "What's going on?"

"I was just thinking that, even though I didn't get the attention I may have wanted from Mom Murphy, I at least had my foster siblings to fill in the gap." He went still, and she filled in the blank... *Who did you have?*

No one.

Her lips tightened, fighting back the old hurt, confusion and anger, willing the first words to stay stuck in her throat. *I was so lonely. So was my depressed mother. Having each other wasn't enough.* Was that all she could promise sweet little Dani?

"Look," he said, obviously reading her expression of withdrawal, "I know you're still upset about my bringing up Fernando."

That was a fact also, but she had new concerns on her mind, which protected her from the ancient feelings threatening to make her break down right then. "Sam, I'm more upset with this Superman complex you seem to have. That you don't understand you can't do everything by yourself."

Sam and Dani's situation was too damn similar to the always-absent father setup when she'd been growing up. Because her father had been doing good things to help other people, she had never been allowed to express her true feelings of loneliness and longing for attention and his love. Nice little girls weren't selfish. Look where it had gotten her mother.

Though Sam was a completely different person than her father, she kept getting tripped up projecting those old awful feelings onto him. And now Dani wanted her to put him to bed every night. He'd told her he loved her. The kid needed a mother, and that was the last thing she thought she could be.

"Dani misses you, that's all I'll say."

He ground his molars and rubbed his temples. "Look, I've just had to tell a mom who brought her four-year-old into the ER last week, thinking he only had a bad flu, that he has leukemia. I had to admit him and get him started on chemotherapy. It's not a Superman complex, it's a job. Now, if you'll excuse me, I need to go give my son a hug."

That did it. *That poor mother.* The dammed-up feelings burst free and Andrea cried. Oh, could she ever have the emotional stamina to be a parent? Sam had seen it all as a pediatrician, he'd spent most of his life in a huge family with rotating foster kids, and though she tried to insist he was being selfish by even thinking about another adoption, the truth was he was anything but. The hard part would be trying to explain all of that to Dani.

She was the emotionally deficient one. She was the one who was selfish. Broken.

They hugged and kissed and comforted each other as no one else could. He wiped away her tears, even as she tried to smile through them. She told him she loved him and he did the same, then she left him for her house, so he could peek in on his boy and give that hug he so desperately needed just then.

Being a parent had to be a killer job. She'd never be able to do it.

* * *

The next night Sam was getting ready to put Dani to bed. The boy had been moody at dinner and throughout his bath. Maybe he was coming down with something. He felt his forehead, looked into his eye, and everything seemed fine, but Dani squirmed and resisted his intrusion.

"Ready for your bedtime story?"

Dani shook his head.

"What? No *Goodnight California* tonight? What about the truck book?"

Dani pouted and folded his arms. "I want Andrea."

To read to him? "She's at her house tonight."

"I want her to put me to bed." That was possibly the longest sentence Sam had ever heard come out of his son's mouth and, boy, had it packed a wallop.

Was his kid mad at him for not being around enough, as Andrea worried about? Or had the boy done the same thing he'd done, fallen in love with Andrea and wanted her there 24/7? Oh, man, this couldn't be good, two guys pining for the same girl. "She'll be back in a couple of days." Fingers crossed that wasn't a lie about the upcoming weekend. "Come on," he said, tickling Dani, hoping to tease him out of his sulking. "Want a bowl of your favorite cereal before I read to you?" No, he wasn't above bribing his kid out of a sour mood.

The offer got immediate consideration. Thank God for children and short attention spans. And endless appetites. "And don't forget you get to see the eye doctor for a recheck day after tomorrow. You need to be big and strong for that, and also get lots of sleep. You don't want the doctor to give you a sleepy eye report, do you?"

The child didn't have a clue what that meant, neither did he, but it definitely got Dani's attention. "No," he said, both his real and prosthetic eye wide.

After Dani had eaten his cereal and magnanimously

allowed Sam to read him a bedtime story and kiss him good-night, he admitted that Dani thought of Andrea as a mother figure. How had he not thought that would happen? Probably unconsciously had wanted it. For a smart guy, sometimes he was a real bonehead. Had he inadvertently set her up to be his competition for his son's affections? That needed to change, unless she was interested in marrying him. The thought sent a little shock down his spine.

He finally got around to eating that sandwich, since the bowl of cereal before with his son had hardly helped quench his appetite. As he chowed down tuna salad on toast, he reran in his mind the entire conversation from earlier with Andrea. She understood loneliness and worried about Dani. She loved his kid as much as he did. Didn't have to say it, it was very apparent. And he himself loved her for a hundred different reasons.

He had proof that she'd wanted him once upon a time, too, since he still carried around the note she'd written him the first night she'd invited him to her bed, sketched winking eye and all. Yeah, he'd folded up that letter the next morning after they'd first made love and tucked it away in his sock drawer for times like these. When he got ready for bed later, he'd pull it out and take a well-needed look.

Seemed as if there was only one way to settle the issue.

Maybe it was time to make their relationship full-time?

The last bite nearly stuck in his throat. Was he ready to risk asking the big question of another woman finding her way back to her artistic passion? Proposing had totally backfired with Katie. But looking back, he realized all the obvious signs with her. Things were completely different with Andrea. He loved her. Trusted her. Wanted to make a life with her. He was pretty sure she'd want the same with him. But, still, maybe they should take things one step at a time.

* * *

Wednesday morning, Sam barreled into the ocularistry and anaplastology department to talk to Andrea about moving in together, not out of convenience but as a definite step forward in their relationship, with the intention of making it permanent not far down the line.

He found Judith, wearing her usual eye magnifier headgear, talking to a young man with scraggly blond hair. The guy moved confidently around the room, making clicking noises.

"I'm pretending to shop," he said, with a wry smile, immediately aware of Sam's entrance.

Pretending? Sam stopped and had to think for a second to realize that the twentysomething man must be blind. If so, his prosthetics were phenomenal. "Don't let me interfere."

"This is Ned," Judith said, smiling. "He's a longtime customer." She stood off to the side, like a proud parent.

Ned clicked more, then turned and nodded to Sam, uncannily nailing where he stood in the room.

"Ned rode his bike over to tell me he wants to change the color of his eyes," Judith said, pride brightening her face.

He rode a bicycle?

"I want to go blue. Tired of brown. Oh, hey, what if I get one blue and one green?" His wide, youthful smile was contagious, if not confusing.

Sam needed to clarify something. "You rode a bike over?"

"Yeah, been riding bikes my whole life."

"He's taught himself something called echolocation," Judith said. "Kind of like a sixth sense for the blind. Too bad not many use it or even know about it."

So the clicking sounds helped him find his way around? Kind of like bats using sonar navigation, bouncing sound waves off objects and pinpointing the location? His interest was definitely piqued. "If your technique works, why don't more use it?"

"Socially annoying," Ned spoke up. "Some folks don't want to hang out with a guy who's always making clicking noises. I call it BurstSonar, by the way. Sometimes it even drives my sighted girlfriend crazy." He laughed. "But she loves me anyway."

Sam couldn't get past the original statement. "You seriously rode your bike to the hospital?"

"Woodman Avenue is mostly a straight shot. I only live a mile away but, yeah, I even do off-road bicycling. Why hold myself back?"

"Ned is a great example of a totally independent sightless person. Lives by himself and does everything the rest of us do," Judith said.

"That's commendable," Sam said, stepping forward to shake his hand. "It's an honor to meet you."

He took his hand as if he'd seen it. "I'm a pretty damn good cook, too, if I do say so myself. Nice to meet you, too."

Amazed at what this guy had accomplished without sight, Sam shook his head.

"Ned is an outspoken advocate for independence of the blind, much to the chagrin of many who think of echolocation as annoying or disgraceful, even. Many of them are other blind people, too."

"Seriously?" Sam thought about Dani, and the horrible potential for him to lose his other eye. Wouldn't he want his son to know freedom and independence like this guy if he became blind?

"Yeah, some of my staunchest adversaries are blind people who think echolocation is offputting." Ned laughed, having said the last phrase as though it had tasted bad. "Like the whole point of life is not to bother other people.

Unfortunately, that's what most blind people learn. That they're an inconvenience. That they are destined to spend their lives dependent on the kindness of strangers, the government and blind organizations looking out for them."

"It's a radical concept," Judith chimed in. "Ned has even started his own coalition to raise money and teach independence to the blind through his technique."

"This is fascinating, and, for the record, I think you should go with one green and one blue. Or get a pair of each and change eye color anytime you feel like it."

"That's a great idea." Ned smiled, as if really considering the suggestion. "Maybe I'll go violet."

They all laughed, but Sam suspected Ned might become Judith's first violet prosthetic-eyed customer.

"Well, it's been great talking to you," Sam said, suddenly eager to get back on track to why he'd come down here. "Judith, is Andrea around?"

"She took the rest of the day off after her appointment with Admin this morning," Judith said, unfazed, gazing happily at Ned. "She's painting. The hospital lobby needs new paintings, fast."

"I see." Sam winced over that expression with Ned in the room.

"And I don't," Ned said, not missing a beat. "But, you know, I've always wanted to try my hand at painting."

The quick levity may have gotten a chuckle out of Sam, but it didn't help the uneasy feeling crawling over his skin. Andrea had made connections and had found a way for her talent to be showcased. He certainly didn't begrudge her success, was happy about the hospital lobby deal, but she'd skipped work today because of it. Maybe it was her way of pushing back at her father?

She had paintings to paint, and a part-time job to hold down. Hell, he'd opened the door for her to showcase her work in the St. Francis Hospital lobby after the remodel.

He should consider himself responsible for her taking the day off. If her art took off, lack of time might force her to make a decision about working at the hospital and helping guys like Ned look sighted, or going full speed ahead with her painting...and kissing this place, and him, goodbye?

His history with the women walking away who meant most to him still managed to step in and keep him insecure and off balance. He needed to get hold of himself. Stop the negative, insecure thoughts. But it was the first thing to pop into his head.

Of course he wanted the best for Andrea, wanted to support her every step of the way, whatever made her happiest.

Sam had big plans he wanted, no, needed to bring up with her today. But she wasn't here. She was home, painting. Having to postpone what he wanted to ask her made his stomach knot and kept the knot tight. Women didn't stick around for him. But what if he showed up at her house with the perfect secret weapon?

CHAPTER TEN

It had been an amazingly productive day. Andrea's arms ached from the nearly nonstop painting. The bright sun had helped make her small workroom ideal during the morning, but by afternoon she had to move outside to her postage-stamp-sized patio for the best light. That had never been a problem before because her painting schedule had been so irregular. Now, however, with a couple of commissioned paintings and, in one case, a cash advance, she needed to paint more and consistently.

Maybe it was time to consider renting space in a real studio. She knew artists who did that, shared studio space to make the rent more reasonable, and once she'd cleaned up she planned to make a call or two.

Someone knocked at her door. She glanced at the clock on the wall—it was six-thirty. Wow, she'd really lost track of time this afternoon. She looked a mess wearing a baggy T-shirt and the oldest, holiest jeans in her wardrobe, probably had as much paint on her face, arms, hands and her clothes as on the canvas, but there wasn't time to clean up before answering the door.

Not bothering to check the peephole on the old thick wooden door, she pulled it open a few inches and peeked around the corner.

"Surprise!" Dani blurted, tickled with himself and clapping.

"Hi!" She dropped to her knees, genuinely happy to see him, put her hands on his shoulders and kissed his chubby cheek.

"You look silly," he said.

"I know, I've been painting." Slowly she shifted her vision from the toddler to the long jeans-clad legs behind him, lifting her gaze until she saw Sam's handsome face looking a little more worn than usual. He'd combed his brown hair neatly, and his piercing blue eyes promised this was a no-nonsense visit. Her pulse fluttered at the sight of him, as it always did. "Hi."

"Hi. You get a lot of work done today?"

"Yes. Come in!"

"Don't know if you've eaten, but I brought you some of that take-out chicken you like with black beans and a side salad."

"How thoughtful of you. Thanks. I'd totally lost track of the time." She stood and hugged him hello.

They all went into the kitchen. "Share?" she said.

"We've already eaten. Thanks."

It felt so formal, and not at all the usual casual, comfortable routine between them. Something was up. She opened the bag and took out a chicken leg seasoned with the usual lime and pineapple juice, oregano, garlic and chili pepper—it smelled so good—and took a big bite. Loving the taste, the tenderness, she lifted her eyes to the ceiling, then, also loving the thoughtfulness from the man she loved, she smiled at him and took another bite.

But he wasn't smiling.

"I was surprised to find out you weren't at work today," he said.

Why did she feel the sudden need to explain, to account for her actions, as if he were her father? She shuddered inwardly at the reference, feeling uncomfortably like her own mother. "I've been keeping up on everything, all the orders at work. I sent off the prosthetics I promised to the people in Cuernavaca last week. Even supplied a year's worth of special adhesive for the ears. I needed to get the cat in the bag, no pun intended, so I could get started on my next project. Hey, guess what, I've been commissioned for some paintings for the new hospital lobby."

"I heard that from your grandmother. Fantastic. I'm so happy for you."

"Thanks. I'm a little nervous."

"It'll be a big break for you, that's for sure."

"So you saw Grandma today?"

"Yeah, I stopped by the department, looking for you."

"Did I miss something?"

"A guy who clicks his way around the world."

"Ned! Isn't he an inspiration?"

"Sure is."

She could instantly tell Sam was done with small talk. He'd come here on a mission, and it was obvious he had something he wanted to get off his chest.

She wanted to love Sam and felt he wanted to love her, too, but regardless of their best intentions their pasts seemed to keep tripping them up, him always keeping a safe buffer zone, and her waiting for him to magically turn into her father. Would they ever get past that?

But the truth was she'd also missed him in twenty-four short hours, and that was a fact. Having finished the small chicken leg, she couldn't bring herself to eat another bite, as something besides hunger crowded out her stomach. Anxiety?

"Dani," she said, "would you like to play with the building blocks?" She'd gotten involved enough with Sam that she'd actually picked up a toy here and there for Dani to keep at her house. Remembering how much he liked his building blocks at his house, she'd bought a set for him to play with here.

He rushed at the chance, and soon sat contentedly in the corner of her living room, building a tower, knocking it down, then building another.

Andrea wiped her hands on a napkin, then glanced at Sam, who was still tense. "What's on your mind?"

"I've been doing a lot of thinking," he said, stepping closer, running his index finger along the curve of her jaw. "Anyone ever tell you that you look sexy with paint on your face?"

She gave a breathy short laugh, but tension took hold in her stomach as she waited for what he'd say next. Though the mere touch of his finger nearly made her lose track of her thoughts. How did he do that?

"I think we both know we love each other." He cupped her entire jaw, leaned in and delivered a delicate kiss to prove his point. Kissing always felt so right with him. "If your feelings haven't changed about me, I'm thinking we should join forces, you know, move in together."

Just move in. Like that.

Disappointed, she stared at him, eyes wide, not knowing how to respond. It certainly wasn't the most romantic proposal—in fact, the more she considered it the more she thought it was far too practical. But the man *was* a problem-solver after all. She had to be honest about what it made her think. "Shacking up out of convenience?" *How unromantic.*

He pulled in his chin, his eyebrows knitted. "No. Not at all."

If this was his idea of solving their problems, it made her angry. "Are you sure you're not just looking for a child-care provider with privileges?" she whispered, so Dani couldn't hear.

He grimaced, reacting to her low blow. "I thought you'd be in a good mood after painting all day."

Was he really that clueless? "I am in a good mood, but you seem to think about love as a business deal. You want what you want and I, well, the same. I love you, but a girl likes a little romance along the way."

He held her upper arms, looked deeply into her eyes. "Are you saying you're not interested in moving in?"

"Look, I do love you, and I love Dani so much I can hardly believe it. But I need to know you want me for me, not just to make your plans work out, but because you *need* me. Sort of like breathing."

"That's a bit dramatic, isn't it?" His comment fell flat, he knew it from the expression she tossed at him. So he tried again. "My plans involve making a life with you."

"Are you sure this isn't about putting all your ducks in a row for adopting more kids?" She narrowed her eyes for emphasis.

"Now who's being unromantic? I came here to ask you to move in, a huge step for us. You may not know it yet but we belong together."

Did they belong together? Him holding on to his secrets, giving the impression he was totally into the relationship but somehow always holding back some deep part of himself. She got it that his behavior was in no small part thanks to his childhood and feeling rejected by his mother, but nevertheless. Her with fears of becoming like her mother, giving up, giving in, lost and lonely on child duty while her husband pursued his profession and ignored the relationship.

Dani had stopped playing with the blocks, Andrea couldn't help but notice. "Dani, would you like a graham cracker and some milk?" Besides, she needed something to change the heavy atmosphere.

"Okay."

She led him into the kitchen and set him at the table with his snack. Then she went back to Sam, who was standing exactly where she'd left him, appearing dumbfounded, as if he already knew how things might work out. She pressed her hands together and placed them by her mouth, as if praying, as she approached.

"I do love you, Sam. I'm flattered beyond belief that you want us to live together, but maybe we're rushing things. The thing is, I need to know that it's me you want, and *need*, that I'm not merely a missing piece to fill that big puzzle you've created in your mind about the kind of life you want." She pleaded with her eyes for him to understand, to not be hurt by her honesty. "Don't get me wrong, it's a great idea. I'm just not sure about right now." Realizing she might have just hurt him deeply, she begged with a stare for his understanding. "We've got to be completely honest and open with each other, right?"

"I've been more honest with you than anyone else in my life."

"And I'm so grateful for that." *Was she so messed up that that wasn't enough?* "But you and your big compassionate heart scare me. I'm worried I'll never measure up to your standards. I don't know if I have the same capacity you seem to for reaching out to all those kids in need." Ironically, she worried he didn't need her anywhere near as much as he needed those kids.

Bewilderment filled Sam's eyes. "But you just said you love Dani."

"Yes, I do, and you, too. But I'm afraid I'll lose myself in your busy life, and I've only just started to find me." She pleaded for understanding with her gaze, her body tense and her feet bolted to the floor.

"How can you worry about losing yourself with me when I want success for you, too? I know how talented you are, hell, who do you think suggested you for the hospital remodel project?"

What? He'd set that up? It hadn't been her dazzling talent that'd gotten their attention? Roiling emotions made her face grow hot. Stupid her for thinking Sam was nothing like her father. He'd gone and done something behind her back, manipulating her life without her approval. *Jerome Rimmer strikes again.*

She nearly stomped her foot. Angry darts shot from her gaze, aiming to hurt. Because it ached to realize he'd misused her trust. "You just said how honest you've been with me, yet you listened on the phone when I crowed about how excited I was about the appointment. You never said a word that you'd set it up." He must have felt so proud of himself, not having a clue how much she'd *needed* to win that one for herself.

She wanted to run away to her studio and slam the door, rather than face the man she thought she loved. The man who'd just halfheartedly tried to fix their problems with an offer that they move in together, and to fix her professional problems by stepping in where he didn't belong. But she couldn't stand the thought of leaving Dani in the kitchen confused or worried. She forced herself to move and went to him. "Dani, honey, I think it's time for you to have your bath and get ready for bed."

"Will you read to me?"

"Not tonight, sweetie, but I promise I will soon. Maybe you can come here and spend the night with me sometime?" She tried to hide the slight tremble in her voice. Tried to keep it from breaking.

Sam cleared his throat at the kitchen entrance. She glanced up and saw total defeat on his face. Hell, he'd just asked her to move in with him and she'd essentially turned him down because she felt his big idea was for all the wrong reasons. He'd taken a risk and she'd shot him down.

"She's right, Dani, it's time to go." Sam said it kindly, but with a hint of dejection. The boy dutifully got down from the chair, having finished his milk and cracker, and took his father's hand. The pressure in her chest seemed to squeeze harder with each beat of her pulse.

Andrea rushed to Dani and kissed him good-night. "Have some fun dreams for me, okay?" He nodded. Then she stood, her heart feeling stretched to near tearing, took a deep breath and looked into Sam's tortured gaze. Words failed her.

He nodded his goodbye, skipped the kiss, turned and took his boy home, giving her the impression he totally didn't understand but knew when it was time to go.

She crumpled to the floor, never more tormented and mixed up in her life. How could she let a good man, a man who loved her and wanted to make a life with her, walk away? She'd sent him away!

Why did everything have to lead back to her childhood and her overbearing father planning every aspect of her life but never bothering to be around as she'd lived that life he'd prescribed? And her withdrawn mother letting her father run roughshod over her and never speaking up for her daughter or herself. Would it be the same with Sam? Why couldn't she believe him when he said he loved her and wanted to live with her, and not assume there was a big catch, that he only wanted her for his purposes, not simply because he loved her?

Because there *was* a catch, a huge one. He wanted her and he wanted that big family that he'd never felt he quite belonged in, and he wanted her to be like his saintly foster mother to make his world right again. Mother Murphy had died, the cruelest form of abandonment. Those were huge shoes to fit into.

Andrea felt she was barely ready for anything beyond loving Sam and Dani. But Sam expected so much more.

She trembled with anger over his foolish and insensitive mistake, but more so with fear that deep down she just didn't have what it took to be Sam Marcus's woman.

Things couldn't have backfired any worse. Sam helped Dani into his car seat, even though his hands trembled. Pain, disbelief and a stew of other emotions kept him from thinking straight. He'd asked Andrea to move in, laid it all out there, and she'd brushed it off. Was that all he meant to her? He'd said he loved her. What did she want from him? Had her father messed her up so much that she couldn't trust his honest feelings? Maybe he should have asked her to marry him, but they obviously weren't ready for that!

Why did he feel so numb? Why had he run to her with a last-ditch plan to keep them together when they hadn't really even broken up, and now it felt as if maybe they were on the verge of ending everything they'd barely started.

Why did he never feel good enough?

Did he really expect her to give up everything she held dear for the kind of life he wanted? He honestly didn't think so, but that was evidently how she saw it. If he could only figure out what she wanted from him, he'd do it. If she'd just given him a clue.

Did she really think she'd lose herself in his life? What about building a life *together*? He wanted what she wanted for herself. Hell, he'd spent twenty minutes talking to hospital administration about the new lobby remodel, encouraging them to brighten things up with pieces of art. Not cheap prints but real art from local artists.

As dumb as Andrea seemed to think it was, he'd given the executive secretary to the hospital CEO her website address to search for samples of her colorful artworks. He'd left the meeting with a grin on his face, and it had been for Andrea. All for Andrea. Now she had a commission for paintings.

But that had totally backfired. Man, had it ever. Did a guy who wanted to take over a lady's life do stuff like that?

Oh, man! That was exactly like something her father would do! Jerome Rimmer would go behind her back and set things up, as if she was a little puppet. No wonder she'd gone ballistic.

He'd screwed up royally just now on just about every level and didn't know how to begin to fix things.

Maybe he just needed to get his son home, to go through their nightly routine, then life would feel right again. But without Andrea he doubted life would ever be the same.

He hoped she wouldn't give up on them—he sure as hell wouldn't. He loved her too much. There had to be a way to work this out. But there wasn't enough time tonight.

As he drove into the garage at his home an image of her face appeared to him. "Maybe, instead of losing yourself with me, you'll come to *find* yourself in a life with me," he whispered. "And maybe I'll finally find myself, too."

CHAPTER ELEVEN

THE NEXT MORNING at the medical appointment, the doctor dilated Dani's eye, made a thorough examination, then had his nurse take him into a dark room to play while the eye medication wore off. Sam sat across from the desk in the office, waiting for the doctor.

The doctor looked grim, and Sam's instinct caused his entire body to tense.

The salt-and-pepper-haired ophthalmologist sat with a loud thump on his chair cushion, like a two-hundred-pound sack of potatoes, and sighed. A sound of defeat. "There are early signs of retinoblastoma in the right eye."

Stunned, Sam may as well have been hit with a two-by-four. He couldn't manage to breathe, his heart stuttered, and gut-wrenching pain for his son filled every part of him. He'd gone through this before, yet this time it felt twice as bad. Was that even possible? His head dropped into his hand, the burden of holding it up suddenly beyond his ability.

"We've caught it earlier this time, Dr. Marcus. We'll get a CT scan and an MRI, go through the staging process and see what our options are."

Sam couldn't think straight. Couldn't begin to string words together.

"Since you don't have any medical history on Danilo—I believe you said his parents are deceased?"

It took every last bit of strength Sam possessed to hold himself together. A simple nod seemed beyond his capability at the moment, but he managed to grunt a reply.

"I can tell you that *bilateral* retinoblastomas are always inherited, and therefore one of Danilo's deceased parents had to have been blind from the same cancer." The doctor continued as if Sam had agreed. "And with hereditary retinoblastoma, we must also be on the lookout for pineal tumors in his brain."

The mounting information tore at every nerve ending in Sam's body. Surely this was how it felt to have his heart ripped out of his chest.

"We have options this time around that we didn't with the last tumor because of the size. Even though before, without his family medical history, we didn't know he possessed a genetic mutation, and we hoped it might only affect one side, we might have handled things differently right off if we had known, but all is not lost. Once I gather the staging information, I'll know for sure if it's small enough to consider chemoreduction."

Sam glanced up at the doctor.

"The chemotherapy will be placed directly into the eye to reduce the size of the tumor. Then we can use laser light coagulation, also known as photocoagulation, to destroy any blood vessels leading to the tumor, starve it and destroy it."

"What about his vision?" Sam finally found his voice by focusing on the doctor's treatment plan.

"We might be able to save his sight."

He'd tossed Sam one tiny ray of hope.

"Our goal in shrinking the small tumor and essentially cutting off its blood supply is to save his remaining vision. All we can do is hope for the best and move forward from here."

"Thank you." They might be able to save Dani's sight. That was what he'd hold on to. That would help him through this horror show.

"We'll line up those tests ASAP and move forward as fast as we can," the stocky doctor said.

"I'm counting on it."

Sam left the doctor's office, seeing Dani playing contentedly in the dim room, and nearly lost it again. He inhaled, forcing himself to keep it together for his son. He walked down the hall, out of voice range, and fished out his cell phone with an unsteady hand.

His first thought was to call Andrea. But they'd had that nasty fight and she'd kicked him out of her apartment last night. And truth was he didn't know how he'd get the words out without breaking down. He needed to stay strong right now. For Dani's sake.

He dialed another number instead.

"This is Dr. Marcus. I need to clear my schedule for the next couple of weeks," he told the administrative nurse for his department. "I have a family emergency."

After a couple of days off, and without a word from Sam, Andrea returned to work, hoping she hadn't blown the best thing in her life. Selling her art only brought so much happiness. In fact, without someone to share the milestone with, it felt pretty damn empty. Paintings couldn't compare to a living, breathing man. Nothing could compare to Sam. She'd missed him and Dani terribly and had also missed being in the hospital, working on her projects for patients. By late last night she'd admitted she'd overindulged in painting for the past couple of days and the results on canvas were disappointing, to say the least.

It was time for a change, a breather from creativity, and ocularistry was the answer. Plus she'd be closer to Sam in the hospital.

Feeling fortunate she had choices in life, she entered the department humming.

Her grandmother met her at the door to the workroom. "I thought you'd forgotten you had a job."

"Not for a second. But I did have some banked personal time off and decided to use it."

Before her grandmother could answer, her father strode through the department door. Andrea went on alert.

"Well, I thought you both should know they've hired an administrative assistant from inside to take over this department. Now, Mom, you'll only need to concentrate on O&A. Hell, you can work part-time, just like this one." He pointed to Andrea. "If that's what you want."

"Well, that's good news, but won't I have to train this administrative assistant?" Judith was all about business before pleasure, probably where Andrea's father had gotten it.

"Of course." Andrea's father looked at her, narrowing his eyes, though seeming far less imposing than usual. "I still can't for the life of me understand why you wouldn't take the job."

"You're the head of cardiac surgery, Dad, you don't have to understand what goes on in this department." *Or inside my head.* She knew her vague answer irked the heck out of him, and she thoroughly enjoyed it.

"You're right about that. I'll probably live a lot longer if I quit trying to figure you out." At last, a feeling they shared. His response wasn't to bristle, as it usually was. It actually seemed as if he just shook it off. Wow. That was a first. "But that's not the reason I came down here." He handed his mother a letter. "This came through Administration, and I thought your grandmother might like to read it to you."

Judith opened the letter and read it out loud.

Dear St. Francis of the Valley Hospital,
The community of Cuernavaca, Mexicali, wishes to thank you and your mission members for helping us in our time of need. You saved lives and helped us get back on our feet.

We are especially happy about the recent packages received by many families with new eyes, ears and even noses. These gifts seem like miracles for so many children. The parents of Jesus Garcia cannot thank you enough for giving him back a normal face.

We hope these pictures say what we cannot in words.

Forever grateful.

Moved by the heartfelt letter, Andrea stepped forward. "May I see the pictures?"

Smiling, Judith dug inside the envelope and found a photo, then handed it to Andrea. It was a grainy group shot of all the children she'd helped. Immediate fond memories, recognizing face after face, made her grin. A second picture remained inside the envelope. Judith took it out, studied it, then gave it to her. It was of a young boy that Andrea remembered well, beaming with pride as he now had both ears and a tip for his nose, and it seemed impossible to tell which ear was his and which had been made by Andrea. Though she knew it was the left one.

"This, my dear father, is why I need to be here in the lab, making eyes and noses, and not becoming one of the suits, running things."

Her father glanced at the pictures, then studied them more closely. "Nice work."

Had he just paid her a compliment? Had Mom started sharing her new medication with him? "Thank you. Now, if you don't mind, I need to show this letter to Sam."

"He's off on a family emergency," Jerome said.

Concern shivered through her. "How do you know that?"

"I just came from the monthly administration meeting, remember? He's been off since yesterday."

Anxiety sliced through Andrea over what the reason was for Sam taking family time off. Part of her plan for coming back to work today had been to invite him for lunch and admit she'd discovered that not only did she love him but she *needed* him in her life. And if his offer was still on the table...

Something must be wrong with Dani for him to take off so suddenly. She reached for her cell phone and dialed his number, walking into a secluded part of the department to talk to him, leaving her father and grandmother to chat.

"Sam? Is everything okay?"

"Oh, hi. Um, yeah. Dani's had a couple of tests and we're just keeping things low-key."

"What kind of tests?"

"A CT and an MRI."

He wasn't exactly forthcoming with information about why Dani had needed those tests. "Is he sick?"

Sam cleared his throat. "The cancer has come back in the other eye."

She gasped, couldn't help it, and spontaneous tears flowed. "I'm coming over right now."

"No. You don't have to. We're working through this. We just need some peace and quiet."

Shaken and taken aback that he'd dismissed her so matter-of-factly, she wasn't sure how to respond. "Uh, okay."

"Okay. Thanks for calling."

Still stunned over the horrible news for Dani, and feeling dismissed by a zombie version of Sam, she let him disconnect and stood staring for a few seconds, wiping the tears from her eyes, her fingers trembling. He didn't want her there.

Hurt wrapped her up and nearly squeezed the air from her lungs. She stood, stuck to the spot, thinking rather than panicking.

She'd spent a lot of time thinking while painting the past couple of days, too, and had figured a few things out. Sam kept her at a distance, even when he'd asked her to move in, by making it seem like a practical decision, having nothing to do with love or longing or—her new favorite word—*needing*. Because that was the missing ingredient she'd discovered while painting. Need.

That was how he'd learned to deal with his personal pain of having a mother who'd left him alone and vulnerable, who'd had to give him up and who had never tried to get him back into her life. He'd grown up feeling an outsider in a big family, always afraid he'd get sent away, pretending to be part of one big happy family but always keeping his distance, watching, waiting for the day to come. His relationship with Katie had proved he wasn't capable of committing until it was too late and the relationship was over.

From where she stood, Sam was repeating history with her. He'd asked her to move in in a halfhearted way, not to get married, and had probably used her "no" as a reason to shut her out now.

Well, he wasn't going to get away with it this time because, unlike Katie, *she* loved him enough to fight for him. For Dani, too. *Oh, God, poor Dani!*

Rather than stand there and bawl helplessly, she grabbed her shoulder bag and marched toward the department door. Her father had left, and Andrea spoke to her grandmother on her way out. "I've got some personal business to take care of. I promise I'll be back tomorrow."

Judith raised her palms. "Like I could stop you? Do what you've got to do. Your job's safe with me—that is, until the new administrator takes over." She winked and smiled, as only a grandmother could.

"Thanks, Grandma."

Thirty minutes later Andrea knocked on the white front door of the boxy mid-century modern home in the hills above Glendale. It seemed she'd first stood at this door a lifetime ago. Sam's house. She'd been nervous then, but right now nothing could compare to the butterflies winging throughout her entire body—even her palms tingled. And her heart, it pounded hard enough to break a rib. She'd never taken a bigger risk in her life, but Sam and Dani were worth it.

Sam opened the door looking haggard and pale. He wore sweats and a ratty old T-shirt. His hair hadn't been combed in a while. "Andrea, I said you didn't have to come over."

"And you thought I'd listen? Sam Marcus, you'd better let me in or I'll roll right over you." Yes, it might seem absurd for a woman barely five feet tall to talk tough like that to a six-foot-tall guy, but right now she believed with all her might that she was capable of taking him down if he gave her any grief.

He didn't crack a smile but he stepped aside, letting her enter. "Dani's taking a nap." At first Sam avoided her eyes, but then those tired blues connected with hers and held on. There was so much pain there it made her ache inside. "Look, Dani and I will work through this together, just like we did the last time."

"How can you look me in the face and say that? Don't I mean anything to you?"

"Of course you do, but things have changed since the other night."

"You mean life got tougher, so you shut out the people you need most?" She'd play hardball if she had to. But, honestly, why hadn't his first phone call been to her?

"Didn't you kick me out of your house the other night?"

"I did, because you were being a bonehead. You asked me to move in—gee, how romantic. And you still don't think you need me. Or anyone, for that matter. You won't let yourself need anyone. But over the last couple of days I've done nothing but think about you and us and our situation.

"Now, are you going to let me sit down and get me some water or do I have to do that myself?"

She wasn't sure where this wild warrior woman had come from, but right now Sam needed someone to tell him what to do, and she was more than happy to do it. She trudged on into the living room and sat down. He brought her a glass of water, and one for himself, and she couldn't help but notice his hand trembled when he set the glass down. Her heart grieved for him in that moment, but she needed to say her spiel and get him to realize a few things before she could let out her true emotions over Dani's heartbreaking situation.

She took a sip for strength. "I say this as one only child to another. You've always felt like an outsider and kept your distance, even from me. Your foster mother loved you unconditionally, but you never believed it because it would hurt too much if she sent you back into the program, like some of the other kids that passed through her house."

"What's this got to do with anything?" He was definitely short on patience, and could she blame him?

"It has everything to do with us. Don't you see? You've always felt like you needed to prove yourself in order to be loved. Dani was abandoned. You knew how that felt. You could help him and return the favor your foster mother did for you. Loving a vulnerable kid is easy compared to a complicated grown-up like me."

She took a long drink to gather the confidence to bring up the next part. The part about her. "Then there's me, a girl who always felt rejected by her father. I didn't have a clue how to trust a guy, and you wanted to keep a safe distance, but the problem was that we had the hots for each other. We were crazy about each other's bodies. So we got in over our heads and tried to be grown-ups doing grown-up things, like falling in love." She'd been looking around the living room instead of at him because what she had to say was hard, but now she zeroed in on him. She had to, to make sure he was following her line of thinking.

"But we still weren't ready for that, even though we're both adults. Then there was the third ingredient of *us*, Dani. He needed both of us because he lost both of his parents. And like I said, you and I really got along great in bed, and we thought we loved each other. Which is fine. We should love each other. But, Sam, there was still something missing. *Need.* We had to need each other, and not just for practical purposes."

She stood, walked to him and knelt down in front of him, placing her palms on his knees. "After you left the other night, after you made the most unimpressive suggestion about moving in together, I had a lightbulb moment. You didn't need me in that deep-down, I-can't-live-with-out-you way every girl dreams about. It felt almost as if you could take me or leave me. Safe. You know?"

He didn't react in an obvious way, but she was quite sure there was a glint of something in his gaze, except she was too afraid to read it just then. What if he really didn't need her? "I had time to think and I realized I truly *needed* you in my life, whether you were ready for me or not. You made me come together. All my mixed-up parts finally came together. I needed you for that. Now I'm here because *you* need *me*. Because the little boy we both love is sick and *needs us* to come together and be there as a family unit for him. And you're right, that might not be any more sexy or romantic than your offer to shack up, but I'll settle for that right now. For Dani's sake."

She glanced up and saw a hint of gratitude in his gaze. "You need me because you don't have the strength on your own to go through this alone again." She squeezed his kneecaps. "You need me, Sam. And because of that I want to be here for you. For Dani." Her eyes prickled, her vision blurred. She'd gotten to the hard part, the part she'd promised herself on the ride over she'd beg for if she had to, and so far it looked as if she might have to. "I'll be your rock, I won't abandon you if things get too tough, I'll be your safe haven, I'll comfort you, I'll love you with everything I've got, because I love and *need* you, Sam." The tears came and she couldn't hold them back. "Can you admit you *need* me?" Her voice fluttered.

The invisible mask that held Sam's face together dissolved. His chin quivered and his eyes squinted tightly, forcing tears out the sides. He grabbed Andrea's hands, squeezing them like a man afraid to let go. "I thought I'd lost you forever when you asked me to leave. I might be the kind of screwed-up guy who asks a woman to move in because it's the practical thing to do, but underneath I meant it with all my heart, and I was too damn afraid to ask you to marry me."

She squeezed his hands. "Say it, Sam."

"Propose?"

She shook her head. "You know what I want to hear."

"I love you, Andrea."

"And I love you. But I *need* you even more. Now say it. Please?"

He grew very serious and stared down at her. "Honey, I need you. I can't face life without you."

She sighed as chills covered her shoulders and back. He reached for her and she climbed onto his lap, wrapping her arms around his neck and kissing his wet cheek. "Baby, I'm all yours."

Later, when Dani woke up, Sam made a simple dinner for the three of them, and afterward they played blocks and trucks and pretended that Dani's life hadn't been turned on its head again, until it was time to put him to bed. They'd take it one day at a time from here on.

"May I do the honors?" Andrea asked.

A week ago Sam had felt threatened by the fact that Dani had wanted Andrea to put him to bed instead of him. Tonight the request seemed like a godsend. How had he been so lucky to find a woman as strong and unyielding as Andrea?

"Give me a kiss," he said to Dani. The scrawny kid's arms circled his neck and tiny soft lips brushed his cheek, giving Sam a little taste of heaven, yet he ached inside. "I love you."

"I love you, too," Dani repeated, oblivious to what the near future would bring, as he trotted off to Andrea's waiting hand. She beamed at the boy who'd soon be facing the battle of his life, but for now he was suspended in sweet grace, surrounded by the two people who loved him most.

As Andrea and Dani walked down the hall Sam couldn't help but overhear his son's question. "Are you going to be my mommy now?"

Andrea laughed. "That's up to your daddy."

Sam grinned, the first time he'd done so since he'd gotten the dreadful diagnosis for Dani's remaining eye. Then he called out, "You can count on that, son."

EPILOGUE

One and a half years later...

DANI JUMPED ONTO the grass from the new wood swing set in the backyard. His independence always put Andrea on edge. He quickly utilized his newly learned skill of clicking to find his way back to the seat and climb on again. He'd been taking lessons from Ned, learning the art of echolocation and future independence, right along with Braille. They hadn't been able to save his vision but had successfully killed the cancer.

At first the blow from the news about Dani having retinoblastoma in his remaining eye had seemed insurmountable. But Andrea and Sam, together, had given each other strength and support so they could be the rock their boy had needed while he'd gone through the process of going blind.

They'd also, as the tight-knit family unit they'd become, agreed not to coddle Danilo unnecessarily. Their goal was to make a stable home for the boys, something they could depend on and trust, and that was now especially important for Dani. That's where the lessons with Ned came in, and the increase in Dani's confidence as a result brought joy to both Andrea and Sam.

With his prosthetic eye in place, and his sightless eye

looking exactly like the prosthetic, from this distance no one would ever notice he was blind. Dani jumped from the swing again, this time landing on his butt and laughing. Fernando may have a prosthetic leg, thanks to the drug cartel blowing up his village, but he ran like the wind, thanks to the latest high-tech prosthetics, and he swooped in to give his little brother a hand. Nando's determination never ceased to amaze Andrea, and he always touched her heart with his gentle spirit. She couldn't imagine a life without either of her sons.

Once Andrea had married Sam, she'd seen how much Sam had helped the orphanage in Mexicali and that he'd always stayed in touch with Fernando's caregivers. Opening her heart to loving and needing Sam had opened her mind, too. She'd been the one to suggest they go through with the adoption. It had taken over a year, but here he was, a great addition to their ever-growing family.

Nando tripped on a tree root as he rushed to aid Dani again, but she didn't run to him. These days it was too hard for her to get up. She and Sam had made a pact that the boys would be as independent as any other kids their age. She and Sam were determined not to let their sons' special challenges hold them back in life. That's why they'd let Nando try out for the junior soccer team in grade school, and he'd been accepted. He knew how to get back up, and he wasn't hurt from tripping just now, so she stayed put in the Adirondack chair.

In the meantime, Dani had found his way to the slide and, squealing with joy and hands held high in the air, he slid down a little too fast, and at the bottom he tumbled head over heels onto the grass. After a long motherly sigh, Andrea watched with interest to see how he'd handle things. He started to stand, but not before his big brother had offered him a hand and pulled him up.

"Thanks!" Dani said. "Did you see that?"

"Pretty cool," Fernando said, with a proud brotherly smile showing the gap from his newly missing front tooth.

Dani soon rushed back to his favorite outdoor pastime, the swing set and jungle gym complete with tree house, clicking all the way to the ladder for the slide. Back up he climbed.

Being eight and a half months pregnant made it almost impossible for Andrea to keep getting up and down. By the time she stood up, Fernando and Dani would have already worked out their problems, and wasn't that the way to raise two independent boys? So she just sat there and observed the fun, praying for the best.

"Dinner's ready!" Sam called from inside their new extra-large home. They'd found the perfect older house farther up the hills of Glendale, bordering La Crescenta, with four bedrooms, an add-on in the basement doubling as an art studio and prosthetics lab, including patient and/or client waiting area. So Andrea could work out of the house part-time for the hospital and part-time for herself. Judith had trained the replacement for herself and was now happily retired, but still working two to three days a week. The new house also had a rumpus room and a huge backyard! How could they raise two boys and their soon-to-be little sister without those essentials? And Grandma Barbara was a frequent guest, especially if Andrea had work or painting to do and Sam was at the hospital. Having grandchildren seemed to make her mother happier than Andrea had ever seen her.

Sam strolled toward Andrea, love openly twinkling in his eyes, and helped her up from the chair, then kissed her gently. She never grew tired of her husband's simple displays of affection. She'd made the smartest decision of her life in marrying him. Once she'd convinced him of how much they needed each other, old emotional walls had come tumbling down and they'd never looked back. Neither had they ever been happier.

"Eww," Nando teased.

"What happened?" Dani asked.

"They kissed. Again."

"Yucky."

The boys giggled, then rushed toward their parents.

"When are you guys going to get used to it?" Sam said, smiling, herding his sons along toward the house, Dani clicking all the way. "Wash your hands!" he called out when they overtook him, beating him to the back door, then he turned back to Andrea. "You coming?"

"In a second." She'd had a Braxton Hicks contraction when she'd been getting up and wanted to wait for it to subside. Using the time to gaze around, she grinned at nothing in particular and everything in general. The yard. The huge oak tree. The beautiful old house. The sky the exact color of her husband's eyes. The family that had just rushed inside for dinner. Her family. The people she loved with all her heart.

To some the life she'd chosen might seem super complicated, and it was, but the strangest thing had happened— she'd managed to find herself in the middle of that chaos. To Andrea the challenge of becoming Sam Marcus's wife had turned out to be the greatest adventure of her life.

* * * * *

MILLS & BOON®

MEDICAL ROMANCE™

THE ULTIMATE IN ROMANTIC MEDICAL DRAMA

A sneak peek at next month's titles...

In stores from 28th January 2016:

- **His Shock Valentine's Proposal** *and* **Craving Her Ex-Army Doc** – Amy Ruttan

- **The Man She Could Never Forget** – Meredith Webber *and* **The Nurse Who Stole His Heart** – Alison Roberts

- **Her Holiday Miracle** – Joanna Neil
- **Discovering Dr Riley** – Annie Claydon

Available at WHSmith, Tesco, Asda, Eason, Amazon and Apple

Just can't wait?
Buy our books online a month before they hit the shops!
visit www.millsandboon.co.uk

These books are also available in eBook format!

MILLS & BOON®

**If you enjoyed this story,
you'll love the the full *Revenge Collection*!**

**Enjoy the misdemeanours and the sinful world
of revenge with this six-book collection.
Indulge in these riveting 3-in-1 romances
from top Modern Romance authors.**

Order your complete collection today at
www.millsandboon.co.uk/revengecollection

MILLS & BOON®
The Billionaires Collection!

This fabulous 6 book collection features stories from some of our talented writers. Feel the temperature rise with our ultra-sexy and powerful billionaires. Don't miss this great offer – buy the collection today to get two books free!

2 FREE BOOKS!

Order yours at
**www.millsandboon.co.uk
/billionaires**

MILLS & BOON®

Man of the Year

Our winning cover star will be revealed next month!

**Don't miss out on your copy
– order from millsandboon.co.uk**

Read more about Man of the Year 2016 at

www.millsandboon.co.uk/moty2016

**Have you been following our
Man of the Year 2016 campaign?
🐦 #MOTY2016**

MAN OF THE YEAR